PLAY IT AGAIN, KAM
THE KAMRYN CADE MYSTERY SERIES
BOOK 1

NAN HAGAN

Hollywood Way
Mystery Press

Play It Again, Kam
The Kamryn Cade Mystery Series, Book 1
Copyright ©2013 by Nan Hagan

Fiction/Mystery/Cozy/Private Detective/Women Sleuths/Comedy/Hollywood
ISBN-13: 978-0-991076-40-6
ISBN-10: 0991076400

Editorial services by Helene E. Hagan
Senior Editor, The Edit Agency, Burbank, CA

Back cover author photo by Gisele Fleury

The Hollywood Way Mystery Press
2140 N.Hollywood Way, #6746
Burbank, CA 91510
www.hollywoodwaymysteries.com

v.ii

Sabrina and Perrey

two amazing actresses
two amazing friends

Thank you for your always generous friendship, faith and support and for graciously and
willingly inspiring so much material for Kam.

Acknowledgments

I wish to thank the following:

My mother, whose lifelong examples of dedication, perseverance and discipline not only impress me, but inspire me. My father, for his never ending support in whatever crazy endeavor I set my compass to. My brother, because he keeps me in clover and my 'sista', Jen, one of my biggest fans and a truly talented writer herself (now get busy with your own book).

Mindy Kanaskie, my oft-times producing partner in Hollywood, for taking this script around for years and championing it endlessly, telling anybody at any network they should make this. The Crew (the Palo Alto posse), everything I know about fun and friendship starts and ends with you. And Molly Whelan, just in time... for listening to every idea and spark and rant and whatever, for the years...

A note about formatting

Play It Again, Kam was originally written as a pilot for a one-hour TV dramedy series. When it came time to novelize the story, I decided to incorporate a few script elements into the series' book design. Instead of chapters, I kept the TEASER/ ACTS/TAG and FADE structural elements common to standard broadcast scripts (act structures are not used in cable scripts). I used SCENE HEADINGS to quickly set or change the scenes or angles of emphasis. I capped the names of new CHARACTERS in the first scenes where they appear and I capped SOUND CUES, just out of habit. What resulted is a hybrid script/novel format that I felt suited the transition of the original material, as well as the book series' Hollywood setting. I hope book readers will enjoy these slight changes to the standard novel format.

Nan Hagan

PLAY IT AGAIN, KAM

TEASER

FADE IN:

EXT. LOS ANGELES – DOWNTOWN – NIGHT

I am not a real private investigator, I just played one on TV—which is why when the GUNFIRE rang out loud, just over my head, ECHOING a PING, PING as it ricocheted off the brick building in front of me, I pretty much freaked out.

Stopping in my tracks, I turn to see who could possibly want to see me dead. And it's then I think, hmm, turning to face your would-be-killer is probably the last thing somebody being fired at should do. But it's too late when I realize this, like so many things.

As the high beams draw closer, I take little really unhelpful baby steps backward, glancing for some miraculous TV escape.

I am filled with a kind of fear that I haven't felt since

I won the People's Choice Award and had to go on stage in a dress that was too long, too tight and impossible to look good in while breathing. There is nothing on sheer terror like a Hollywood award show, broadcast to millions, just waiting for you to fall on your ass, which, for the record, I did not.

I somehow floated up, flawlessly, was the picture of the perfect TV idol.

I have always known, when the camera is on, I can do anything. It's when the camera's off that I have problems.

The high beams creep over me. I reflectively raise my arm to shield my eyes and wonder if, given the distance, they can actually see me.

The engine REVS and the car speeds toward me like a death missile. That answers that.

As I turn to run, I catch the outline of a sweet, vintage convertible Cadillac coming at me, on an angle.

Did I mention, I'm on the sidewalk? This obviously is not going to offer me the safety I had been counting on.

I'm not sure exactly what clicks in me, but I find a second gear I didn't know I had. I suspect it's the thought that I haven't yet won the Emmy for *Outstanding Lead Actress in a Drama Series* that Madame Sazamora's tarot cards predicted I would. I know it's petty, but I'm not dying until I get that, not if I can help it.

Desperate for divine intervention, I think about the wisdom of *The Secret* which instructs me that I can do anything if I simply focus my desire. So I scrunch my face and focus, hard, in an all-body effort to unlock my inner power reserve to supercharge my way the heck out of this. But let's get real. They have a car. I'm on foot. So, unless the secret is I'm actually Jamie Somers, they're going to catch me.

I'm finally forced to admit what I feared all along: *The Secret* is a sham. I vow, if I live another day, to apologize to all the members of my extended family down in Georgia, for whom I bought the book for one Christmas and not-so-subtly implied that their tendency to obesity was caused by their lack of true desire to reach their higher selves (honestly, I meant well).

But that's beside the point at the moment, because the Caddy sails up alongside me and a Shrek-like-goon (big, not green), who's standing in the backseat, belly up against the door behind the driver, reaches out and *grabs me!*

As soon as I'm airborne in SHREK's grip, I wonder why I didn't run a little farther away from the edge of the curb. Seriously.

The driver, a little ferret-of-a-man, Yin to Shrek's Yang, jams the speed and lurches the vehicle, which SQUEALS as it changes course.

My feet sway in the breeze. I will never again parrot the idea that being swept off one's feet might be romantic. I can now say, with authority, it's frightening.

Fortunately, it doesn't last but a beat, as Shrek re-adjusts his handle on me and heaves me, ragdoll like, into the backseat. I fly akimbo-style and land in a not very lady-like position.

"Hey, now. Ouch." I attempt to sit upright, drawing myself as far away from the big guy as I can get.

"Fatman wants to talk to you." Shrek's voice was deep, pleasant. I wonder if he's ever considered doing voice over work.

"Oh, now come on... You're not really that fat," I say. I hate it when people self-criticize.

Shrek looks at me puzzled. The ferret-man driver snickers.

"Not me. Fatman." Shrek thunders. He then startles me by slapping me across the face, *not* TV stunt-slap, but a real slap, the kind that whips your head, dizzies you. I realize, I've actually never been really slapped and I don't like it.

"Wow. That really hurt. Really. I hope you don't plan on doing that again. I mean, physical force never solves anything."

"You're gonna tell us how to do our jobs? Do we tell you how to act?" FERRET throws me a disapproving look in the rearview.

Ignoring it, I smile at him through the mirror, excited, and brighten. "You know I'm an actress?"

"Sure. Everybody knows Kamryn Cade. That *Polly & Jake, PI,* I loved that show. Used to watch it with my mother."

I am overcome with regret that I judged Ferret so harshly for his unfortunate looks. He's obviously a nice enough fellow.

Shrek swats at Ferret, "Don't encourage her."

"No... Go on. I could use some encouragement." I ease into the back of the car, rubbing out my jaw that still stings. "So are you two guys like some crazy fans of mine or something?"

Ferret laughs in that strange Smedley-way again, then: "This is business. Sorry."

"Sorry... Why?" And really, I don't at first get why. I

am weirdly optimistic by nature. I still think there's a chance, whatever this is, it might not end so terribly for me. Years of auditioning for parts I didn't get have taught me to believe strongly in the art of possibility. I have to keep faith. There's nothing to giving up hope.

Shrek responds to my rather naive question by smashing a monster hand on my face. "This is why."

In one motion, he rolls and jabs me in the butt with a thick, nail of a needle.

"Ow, mother fuh..." is all I can muster before a Snuggie-like warmth envelops me and my mouth decides it's not able to finish that final word.

As Shrek releases me, I roll back and commit to the car fully, laying face up to the sky, becoming one with the leather. I may be drooling.

Ferret runs a red light, zooming through a deserted intersection. I glimpse a blue and white street sign hanging from a stoplight arm that reads: *Hope St.* It whooshes by in a blink and then everything goes dark for me.

I'm not quite so out of it that I don't recognize that as some sort of symbolic foreshadowing.

FADE OUT.

END TEASER

ACT ONE

FADE IN:

(2 Days Earlier)

INT. B! ENTERTAINMENT - STUDIO – DAY

Oh my god, you're Polly Parker." A blonde woman, who looks vaguely familiar, is coming towards me, hands crossed over her heart, as if she cannot believe her good fortune to see me in the flesh. I love that reaction, miss it, actually.

"Yes, hi." I say, extending my hand toward her.

She doesn't take it. Instead, she moves one of her hands to her mouth in a mock gasp. "I mean, I'm so sorry, Kamryn Cade."

"One in the same." I say with just a hint of my native southern accent sliding through (it does that sometimes). I know the expression really is 'one and the same,' but something about the 'in' seems particularly well-suited to the whole dual-identity part of me and Polly. And I never mind when people see us as one being.

In truth, I kind of do as well, and I know, that is a topic for me to work through with a professional, at some point in my life…

"I just loved you as Polly," she seems truly sincere.

"Me too." I'm unashamed to be so obviously taken with myself. I was good. I know it.

I've just arrived on the set of B! Entertainment's *Where Are They Now?* and the blonde who seems genuinely kerfluffled by me is CASSIDY McCLAIN, the 20-something, rail-thin, perky-cutey pants host of the show my agent affectionately referred to as: *the one for the god-damned forgotten losers of years gone by…* (I left out a few f-bombs, but you get what he means).

I'm told it'll be just a few moments before we take our chairs in the middle of a replica (I think) of my old home set, the detective agency's main office, complete with three of the fly-away walls in place. While I was prepared to be on this set today, it still unnerved me a little bit to see it. This fake office feels so real, just like the real fake office of all those years ago.

The memories flood back. And even though I know they're not still there, I'm compelled to walk over to my office doorway and see if any of my usual marks are on the floor, near the area I would lean, just so, casually, as if we hadn't spent twenty minutes blocking action and another thirty lighting me to dreamy, sweet perfection.

Surrounding the rear area of the set, in a semi-circle, backed by a stark, black diorama are a half-dozen or so life-sized PR stills of Michael and me as the characters Polly and Jake, which, if I haven't mentioned, was also the easy to remember title of our show, *Polly & Jake, PI.*

In the center graphic, I'm in my trademark Fedora, holding my trusty *.38*. In another, I'm in a jockey's outfit. In another, a geisha girl's do. In a fourth, a race car driver's uniform. And so on. One of the gimmicks of the show was my nutty, kind-of-a-stretch, weekly turn at some undercover assignment married with Michael's capable constancy as the agency straight man. It was cutely done, or at least so I thought.

And since we were number one in our timeslot for three years, I can safely say, others thought so too.

By year four, we were apparently less cute and by year five, an unmitigated disaster, in all ways. I'm still bummed with Michael. Honestly, I never understood why he left me.

Sure, he was never really an actor and he pretty much hated the whole Hollywood thing, but come on, why would somebody walk off a hit show? And then to never take my calls for years after, heart-breaking.

After Michael walked, the network decided, unwisely, to go on with just me in the lead, *Polly, PI.* I'll sum up for you how that went: A big bowl of wrong.

I try to be philosophical about my fall from TV stardom. I'm attempting to embrace it with my full heart, as a necessary part of my existence, evolution, whatever... I believe in the Universe having a plan for all of us. I'll admit, I'm not thrilled with mine, currently, but I'll go along with it and until something breaks. Something always breaks. You just have to hope it breaks your way.

A window on one of the fly walls SLAMS down with

a THUD and rattles. I stare at it. A bad omen. Yeah, I believe in omens too.

"You okay?" Cassidy has appeared at my side.

I nod, refocusing on the moment.

"You know, we get buckets of mail every day begging for a *Polly & Jake* reunion. Never stops."

"Too bad," I say. "But you know Michael... He never does interviews."

"Yeah, about that. Look, quick check, those rumors of bad blood between you and him?" Cassidy pulls her mike wire immodestly through her blouse, clips the lav mike to her collar.

I knew this was coming. This is a constant wonder among the fandom. "No truth to it at all. Tabloid junk."

"No weird, not even a little unresolved something, something?" She inquires, all wide-eyed and TV-scandal-ready.

I shake my head, nixing that idea entirely.

"Great. Fantastic." Cassidy smiles, turns to the Floor A.D. "Is he here?"

"On the move." He points to the studio double doors. All eyes follow. A buzz goes up in the studio.

And I fixate on the *'he'* of *"is he here..."* Because wow, no... but, but... He never does interviews.

In a surreal slow motion, Cassidy turns to me, "We were going to do separate sit-downs because everybody thought you two hated each other. But since there's no hate... Oh, hang on, we want to catch this live..." Cassidy looks to her main camera. The light box on top glows red.

My heart catches and I stop breathing.

"Polly and Jake together again. For the first time since he walked off the set at the end of Season Four. Or was he pushed? Hmm. Today we get the answer that fans of *Polly & Jake, PI* have been waiting years to hear. Kamryn Cade, Michael Barlowe, right here, right now. Live on B! We are so the coolest channel on television."

The main doors open, cameras swing and catch MICHAEL BARLOWE in the flesh. Oh, his sandy, brown hair still tousles up nice. He's clean shaven, which I like on him. He's got a great jaw line. And his blue eyes… I hope they still sparkle when he laughs. I'm surprised, which is silly really, but he's aged in the years since. And of course, he's less, well, Hollywood-polished. That lean and tight, super-cut model look, the standard one-day unshaven in a leather jacket thing, that was all marketing (and did it ever work) and he hated it, well most of it, I guess he stuck with the leather jacket part. Might as well stay with what works.

I exhale and realize how I feel about seeing him, still such a sexy beast.

Michael is momentarily made unsure by the cameras, the rush of people around him. He wasn't expecting this. Big mistake. He hates surprises, almost as much as he hates me. He looks at the studio, the life-sized PR stills, the set and then, his beautiful blue eyes stop on me, and narrow and I get the sideway glance, like it's just too painful to look straight at me.

Yeah… It's not a good reaction.

Cassidy moves to him, "Michael, you delicious thing. Come over here."

Michael gives me the laser death stare I suddenly

remember so well.

He ignores Cassidy's invitation to join her on set. Instead, he turns, pushing a cameraman out of his way, knocking a floor camera, sending it crashing into another and exits out a side door, leaving chaos in his wake.

It's all surprisingly hugely dramatic, which is ironic coming from Michael, who is *Mr. No-drama*, or at least he would like to think he's that guy.

Cassidy looks to me.

"Yeah, okay, maybe there's a little something, something unresolved."

I bite my lip, my signature bit of cute business and think... What would Polly do?

EXT. RED GARLAND STUDIO – ON MICHAEL

What was she doing there? I was told she'd never do that show. Why am I surprised? People in Hollywood lie.

As I cross the Red Garland Studios lot, in the white heat of valley sunshine, I pull out my sunglasses, hide behind them, and eye the rows of side-by-side, hangar-sized boxes, framed by blue sky and the desperate, water-starved foothills of nearby Griffith Park.

I remember the first time seeing stages, dopey-eyed, in awe of their vast emptiness and their easily transformed interiors. Back then, it seemed like a good thing that something could change so quickly, so completely, be filled with so much make-believe you could literally lose track of what was real and what wasn't.

Now I know better.

Nothing good or decent comes from all this make-believe. If I sound bitter, it's because I am. I have been since the day I walked off the set of my show.

My show. A show based on me.

Here's the backstory of it: My grandfather dies, leaves me his detective agency, a little hole in the wall, overlooking Venice Beach. I'm in college studying who-cares, I-don't-know-what, and suddenly I'm a licensed private investigator. I solve a few cases. I meet a few girls. Turns out I'm good at it and I look good doing it. One of the girls is a publicist, who knows somebody who knows somebody at *Rolling Stone*. I'm branded the *New Era of LA Cool*.

I know this is fleeting and meaningless and yet, I let them. I enjoy it. I sell it to them. And the biggest mistake of my life: I agree to star in their ridiculous version of me.

I hardly have a right to complain about this. Say what you want about Hollywood, they pay. And after they buy your soul, you gotta just shut up and take it when they walk all over it. But you can be mad about it, apparently, for years.

EXT. RED GARLAND STUDIO – ON KAMRYN

My '*What would Polly do?*' led me to the obvious:
Give chase. So I grabbed my white, three-quarter length
down coat off the makeup chair and ran, much to the shock
of the entire *B! Where Are They Now?* crew. I'm pretty sure
they tried to follow. I heard a big CLUNK behind me, a floor
camera, probably, stuck in the doorframe of the side door
Michael and I escaped out of.

I don't miss a step at all as I move from studio to
asphalt. I'm thrilled on all accounts to be flying through Red
Garland in my four-inch Louboutins. Running in insanely
high heels isn't so hard once you get used to it. I'd forgotten how fun it feels. Polly did a lot of running and since
Michael's so tall and I'm not at all, that was usually in the
pretty sticks.

"Michael. Wait." I scamper up toward him. He looks
back, but doesn't stop. It's so Michael and so irritating.

"Hey…" I scream insistently and I move a little
faster, coming around in front of him. "Come on."

"Go away, Kam." He surprises me by changing direction abruptly and heading down a deserted street, on the far end of the lot.

Determined and not in the mood for anything that smacks of rejection, I move faster and catch him. I put both my hands on his chest, leaning my hundred or so pounds into his 180 something (maybe 190 now) and I dig my heals in, cartoon-like.

He could easily knock me over if he kept his pace. He doesn't. He stops, fixes a look on me and doesn't flinch, doesn't pull away. I smile, momentarily distracted by the thought of: Wow, his chest is still really fantastic…

"What are you doing?" He throws me that look, that mocking look that cuts me to the bone, so easily knifes through my sunny façade.

"Trying to get you to stop."

"Okay. Now what?"

Bad timing, but I draw a blank.

"Typical, Kam…You have a grand plan, but it's never thought out."

"Don't be mean."

He takes me by each wrist and removes my hands from his chest, not fast and not with anger. It's weirdly electric to have his hands on me like that. I didn't expect it. He lets go, takes a step back from me. There's a beat, then.

"You're not a little bit happy to see me? I'm happy to see you." I say, cajoling. Michael used to be cajolable. "How can you still be mad? Doesn't it help that the show completely bombed after you left?"

"Sure. Reaffirmed my faith in the cold, cruel world."

I'm surprised how stung I am. "I didn't expect you to be so thrilled with my crash and burn."

Michael looks away. I suspect he doesn't want to be sucked into being nice to me. He gets uncomfortable around emotion. I try to use that to my advantage.

I reach out my hand, put it gently, firmly on his forearm. "You don't think maybe the Universe wants us here, together? Like this, right now?"

We share a look. His says: Me-so-crazy.

"I'll forgive you for being mean if you take me for a cup of coffee. Or tea, because, you know, of course, I don't do coffee. And I would prefer someplace like Priscilla's or Hugo's. And, it would have to be later. I have an audition at Warner's in about an hour. Can you wait before you go back over the hill?"

He just stares at me.

"I reject your negativity."

"I haven't said anything."

"I can feel it. And I reject it. Just an hour. Please?" I tilt my head in what I think might be my most adorable way.

He reaches out and puts his hands on each of my shoulders, squares me up, holds me firmly, gives me a look I can feel down to my toes.

"How are you? You look good."

His being so close to me unnerves me a bit, in a good way, and I'm confused by his sudden friendliness.

"You feeling a little vulnerable?"

I nod. I really am.

"You need to know I don't hate you."

I nod again. "I really do."

"And you need to know that I don't think you're a bad person."

"It has bothered me all these years." He so gets me. He always did.

"I know how much you need to hear these things from me, Kam, and I just want you to know, I'm never, ever, going to say them to you."

"Michael." I gasp, so surprised at his evil trap.

"I'm glad we had this little talk. We've needed it. And now we're done. Let us be done, okay?"

I think maybe I might be tearing up. I just nod and look down as he starts to walk away.

"I don't want us to be done," I yell at him, because I never seem to let anybody get the last word on me.

He stops, turns, comes back towards me, embracing me, like a lover he just can't let go of.

"I knew it. You don't really hate me."

He leans into me, brushes the hair away from my ear and whispers: "I do, Kam. Someday you'll get over it. But for right now, does your phone have a camera on it?"

"Of course. Doesn't yours?"

"I left mine in the car and actually, no. It's just a phone, not some stupid, trendy, hipster, pocket computer doubling as a lifestyle badge."

"Oh," I say, as I pull my stupid, trendy, hipster, pocket computer doubling as a lifestyle badge out of my pocket and hold it up for him to see. "Like this?"

"Exactly like that. I knew you'd have an iPhone. Let me have it…"

He tries to take it from my hand, but I pull away, give him a curious look.

"Won't your hand melt or something if you touch an Apple product?"

"I just want a picture… of you. To remember this by. It's a moment, right? And you love moments." He smiles. But his acting chops are rusty and his heart's not in it.

"I do. That's true. But Michael, at best, you hate moments. I'm pretty sure you are hating this one. So… what's really going on here?"

"Just give me your phone." His smile fades back to his usual, snarky grimace.

I hold the phone with one hand and tap the camera button bringing the app on. "How about I take a picture of you, instead?" I have him in a great shot. I don't take it because I know he wouldn't like it and I try to respect that for people. I know that just because I love to Instagram my life around the ether, doesn't mean others are the same place on that and especially Michael. He doesn't like pictures much, which is weird, because he's a man who looks super hot in almost any freeze-frame.

"You can't just let me do this one, simple thing?"

"Do you even know how to use this? If I remember, you are not exactly Mr. Techie."

"And now I remember, you make everything so hard. Forget it." He turns to go.

"Michael. If I promise to get those two Feds who are watching, will you tell me what's going on?"

I don't turn around, I don't give any indication that I am interested in the two men across the wash. They're about

200 yards from us, on the other side of a chain-link fence, parked at the edge of the cement-snake river wash which is ironically, or maybe aptly, called the LA River.

The guys watching us are dressed like Jake and Ellwood Blues and are pretending to be tourists interested in the studio backlot. But really, they seem to be doing nothing but taking long-lens pictures of Michael and me.

Momentarily I think, maybe they're TMZ and how great this would be to be pictured with Michael. But then again, if they're catching this sound, how humiliating for me. Fame can really be just so complicated sometimes. And besides, I know, TMZ is not interested in me. So, they're Feds, for sure.

"Are you on a case? Why would Feds be following you?"

Michael's eyes flit from the Blues Brothers then to me.

"What makes you think Feds?"

"A vibe." I slink around him playfully and click a picture. To the black hats across the way, we appear to be two old-friends goofing with each other.

I come up next to him to review it. He looks, as expected, super great. The camera loves him, every angle. I pinch and zoom in on the guys in the background.

"See. Safety snaps on their holsters. Handles look like Glocks. Check it out…" I pull the picture over to the younger of the two men, the one holding the camera to his face (who does that anymore?).

With his arms raised, we get a good look at his holstered weapon.

"Shorter handle." I smile to Michael, who doesn't get it. "Standard issue is a nineteen, this kid's carrying a seventeen. He's fresh out of the academy, not yet used to the bigger gun. Probably has a problem with recoil."

"Wait. Why does that sound so familiar?"

"Episode three-dash-seventeen (that code is our production number which simply means the seventeenth episode of our third season), *The Case of the Quicksands of Quantico*. We went undercover at the academy, busted up a ring of diamond smugglers. Remember? We got to weapons-train with real agents."

"Did you just quote a line from our show?" He sounds so appalled.

"I have that thing, remember? I never forget anything I've read." I beam, proud of this quirky skill of mine.

"No wonder you're nuts. I'd have to shoot myself if I couldn't forget all those stupid lines they made me say. Email me the pic. Delete it from your phone." He places a card in my hand, turns and walks away.

"Are you in some kind of trouble?"

"Trouble is my business," he says without a trace of humor. He actually talks like this sometimes, unaware how right out of the pulps he can be.

"How very Bogey of you. Should I be worried?"

"Only about your career."

I just give him a look. I mean really, how many cheap shots is he going to take at me today?

"Not your business, Kam. Leave it alone." He moves off briskly and I watch. I always liked the way he moved, still do.

"Hey. What are you doing way back here, anyway?"

This stops him in his tracks. He turns slowly and with a controlled, slow-burn look of super-pissed off: "This is the Visitor's Lot. But you're at the stage, right? Rock-star parking. Maybe even your name on a sign." He says this as if it's a crime.

"I didn't ask for it. They just gave it to me."

"I've heard that before, haven't I?"

He fires a cannon ball of a look my way and it hits me full in the chest, in the heart.

He is never going to forgive me.

EXT. WARNER BROS. STUDIO – LATER

Pulling into Lot G, VIP Parking at Warner's, I'm still obsessing about my run in with Michael. Audition days are hard enough without the added anxiety that I'm thoroughly hated by someone who used to be very special to me. And man, he looked good. I'm not used to being hated, disliked in any way. It throws me.

I'm always nervous at auditions nowadays, wondering if my prepared take on the material is what they're looking for. Every audition is a risk. You make a choice how to play it and you just hope your choice doesn't suck.

I take note at this moment that I haven't booked a job since the year after *Polly, PI* went on 'hiatus'. It would just be such so awful if my last IMDb listing (that's the Internet Movie Database, the online bible of actual industry credits) is for a one-named character, guest spot the WB's *Swaying Palms*.

As I prepare myself to go in, I feel the panic welling, do what I can to keep it hidden.

INT. KAMRYN'S CAR – SAME TIME

I look in the rear-view and primp my hair, which is long, full, wavy (unless I have it ironed out) and chocolate-dark. I got lucky with the hair, which I thank my mom's side of the family for. It's one of my best attributes.

Right now, it's pinned up loosely by taking my own strands of hair and braiding them together, a sort of tie-back look, I guess. Stylized casualness, my hair-girl might say. I'm not displeased with what I see. I smile, nothing in the teeth. All good.

I decide to go big and throw on a stylish (I think) Kaboodle Page Boy hat, wisping out strands of my hair to frame my face, just so.

I'm actually feeling pretty today. That's a plus. I'm certain it's because of Michael. Despite the awfulness of the interaction, there was something in the way he looked at me that made me feel he still thinks I'm attractive. Even if I'm making it up, I'll take it. I need that shot of confidence, real or imagined. I can make either work.

EXT. WARNER BROS. LOT – CONTINUOUS

I hop out of the car, working it. I know my favor-ite, form-fitting *Rich & Skinny* wedge-biker, bootcut jeans won't let me down.

Because the *B! Where Are They Now?* interview com-pletely fell apart, I had time to go home and change into a more appropriate 'en-semb' for this part. That was one stroke of luck already (before auditions, I always try and focus on the positives).

I now have on a double-layer tank thing happening on the top, a neutral color over a splash of deep fuchsia. It's a look I consider modest, yet sexy. And as usual, I have on a down coat. This one is short, latte-coffee brown with a fur lining. Very cute and I think just the thing I need to get me off on the right foot in this audition. You'll see.

I never wear tons of jewelry or makeup and I don't have any visible tattoos. Part of my appeal has always been your typical girl-next-door.

I learned long ago not to fight type. Nobody in TV land wants that unless you are a known Meryl Streep which for TV, I guess, means Glenn Close. I'm not either. I'm Kamryn Cade. That's actually a type they call for. You know, Kamryn Cade from years ago.

I head over to Building 12, where the casting office is for this project. Here goes nothing (everything).

INT. CASTING OFFICE – A MOMENT LATER

I enter quietly, because you always want to slip in unnoticed (and never do). All eyes of the girls sitting in the chairs instantly look up to see the new person, to see who might be competition.

You can't help it, but you scan them as well, to check them out, admire their outfits (or not), to see if you actually know anyone in the room. Usually you do. We tend to get called in, in batches of similarities.

Today I can tell instantly, it's a Kammie Cade call. They are all versions of me when I was younger. And I can tell many of them recognize me. They sit up. Eyes go wide, then get controlled and return to their sides while peeking over the top to watch me as I approach the assistant's desk to announce myself and sign in.

They won't approach me unless I indicate I'm open to chatting with them. Unwritten rule in town is, you don't speak to the more famous person first unless they indicate they're in the mood for it.

"Hi, Kamryn Cade." I say to the assistant, a pleasant-looking, pudgy girl. I bend down to sign in.

"Oh my god, of course. Sergio was so excited you wanted to come in for this."

Sergio is the Casting Director on this pilot and my dear, very good friend.

"Anything for Sergio. And I like the role. It's a little out there. Interesting." I smile back.

"Do you have your sides?" She's eager to be helpful.

"Did anything change from what was emailed?"

The assistant shakes her head. Nothing.

"Then I'm good."

"You're going in off book?"

She means without pages, memorized. That's hard for a lot of actors in auditions. Honestly, for me, it's super easy, that memory thing. So I'm not impressed with myself, but I don't mind that the pudgy assistant is impressed with me.

"I hope you don't mind if I say this…"

I don't. I won't. I know what's coming.

"But I just loved you as Polly Parker."

"Thank you. Polly was great, wasn't she?"

The assistant nods, thrilled at this little exchange.

You have no idea, I'm telling you, Polly was a big hit, a cultural touchstone.

The door to the main room opens. There's a light smattering of enthusiastic producer-clapping and friendly banter between the producers and the actress who just auditioned. This sort of thing brings dread to those of us waiting outside. You can see us shift nervously and worry visibly.

The actress, a woman who, I am pleased, does not look that much like me (she's taller, blondish) strides past confidently. Her stressful day is over. In a minute, she'll be on the phone with her agent telling him or her that she thinks she nailed it. Lucky.

Sergio comes to the door and he sees me. "Kammie, candy cane, my sweet treat." He crosses right over and hugs me tight. "You look fabu."

"Oh, Sergio, I love you. Thank you for bringing me in."

"You're my girl. This role was written for you." He smiles and I almost believe him.

"I'm going to take you straight in. You ready?"

I nod. As I'll ever be.

INT. THE ROOM – CONTINUOUS

As we enter, Sergio closes the door behind us and then takes his seat at the far end of the room, with five other men who are seated behind a long, cheap, utility table, with headshots (of all the actresses who've been in here before me) strewn about.

"Gentlemen, this is the fantabulous Kamryn Cade, better known to many of you as Polly Parker."

Sergio warms up the room for me, which is good, because this group is cold, not friendly in any way.

"That was a long time ago, Sergio." I am simultaneously trying to appear humble and working it cute a little bit.

"Then you are due for your next series."

"Well, from your lips to the director's ear."

The room gives a general CHUCKLE and I know this is the moment. I remove my coat, dramatically, revealing my very firm, nicely-toned, yoga body. The men sit up, immediately want to like me more.

Yeah, I know, cheap trick, right?

Are you kidding? I know actresses who do reads without underwear. I can assure you, I'm wearing some, not much, but enough to call home and talk to my mom and not be ashamed of my day. I am definitely going to play this game to the best of my ability. And like it or not, being appealing in television is a super, big part of the game.

"Whenever you're ready."

Sergio will be reading with me (all the parts that aren't my character's).

I nod and then…, go for it, throwing my soul in, whole-hog, as we used to say down where my people are from. "Give me your ignition card." I say with great urgency.

"Captain's grounded you. You have a concussion."

Sergio reads this pretty straight. Casting people don't 'act', they read flat. It's up to you to bring the right tone to the room. That is, in fact, what they are looking for. Do you get the script, the part?

"I'm fine." I stand straighter, conveying my fineness.

"No one falls off a hover and is fine. It was luck you landed on that nun."

"Not for the nun." I look away, fighting back the appropriate emotion one might feel when landing on another human being. "The look on her face, I'll never forget it. I have to stop the Puzzler from blowing up the planet, if for no other reason, for that poor, crushed, girl of God."

I am entirely serious in this read and it is now, unfortunately, that I realize the dialogue, the scene, are not.

I figure this out by reading the utterly astonished faces of the men in the room. It's clear what they're thinking: Wow. Bad. Really bad.

My heart sinks and the next few minutes where I'm forced to go on and finish, regardless of the humiliation for having gotten this so wrong, is just gut-punch awful.

I do not get a goodbye hug from Sergio when it's over.

INT. KAMRYN'S CAR – MOMENTS LATER

I cry big, sobbing, gasping for air, kind of crying. I'm sitting in my car, wallowing, in what I think, hope, is some sort of car-provided cone-of-privacy when…

"What's the matter, Kammie, star-chart off today?"

I look up to find ALAN smiling down at me through the open space where my hard-shell top would be if I had chosen to go out with it today.

My car is a classic, Mercedes 280 SL, which means it's low and Alan, even at just five-foot-eight is still able to loom over the driver's side, as cute and boyish as ever, even more so with the sprinkling of gray that is starting to salt and pepper his hair.

"As a matter of fact, Alan…" I say, while choking back tears, "My planets are in alignment today. Jupiter's in my second house. Saturn's in the fourth. You know what that means?"

"You have too much time on your hands?"

He grins in that way that always made it impossible to get mad at him.

Alan Barnes is my ex-husband, the writer/producer from my show. Our marriage was short and passionate and ended well, considering that for that last bit, we couldn't actually stand each other. Now, a few years removed from the drama of a messed-up union, we genuinely like each other again.

"Be nice. I just tanked another audition."

He makes a face, feeling for me. He opens the car door and indicates for me to get out. I do. And once out of the car, Alan wraps his arms around me and gives me a big, supportive, wonderful hug.

"You just get nervous, that's all."

After we pull apart, I feel better. I just needed a meltdown. I don't deal with stress that well, so I'm prone to crying. You get used to it if you spend any time with me.

"Hang in there. Something'll break for you."

I think right now, I could fall in love with him again. He was always such a voice of faith in me.

"You know, I haven't worked in five years. I've become *Where Are They Now?* material."

"Oh, Kam, no. You didn't." He makes a cringe of a face.

"I did. Apparently my need to be on camera is greater than my dignity."

He looks at me like I'm totally pathetic and I guess, as I say this, I realize I am. And since misery loves/needs company...

"Michael was there too."

This surprises Alan. "Mr. I-Don't-Do-Interviews?"

"I know. So weird. But in the end, we didn't actually do any interviews because as soon as he saw me, he couldn't run fast enough. And then I ran after him and then he wouldn't talk to me and there was this thing with like the FBI watching him or something..."

"What?"

"Or CIA, maybe. Definitely Feds. He's on a case, I guess. Whatever, point is, we didn't talk."

"Okay. Good."

"Why?"

"I just meant, you know, why get into all that? Long time ago. It's the past. Probably better left there." Alan shrugs, suspicious like.

"Why is it whenever the topic of Michael comes up, you always seem suddenly a little bit evasive?

"Am I?"

"Little bit."

Another shrug of evasion.

"What is it? You could tell me now, can't you?"

"Sure. Why not? I never liked the way he looked at you… or kissed you. As your then husband, it got me."

"Oh, Alan, that was just the show…"

"Maybe. But Michael's not an actor." Alan gives me a look.

There was something more with Michael and me and he knew it then, knows it now. And he's not wrong. During the first years of filming *Polly & Jake*, Michael and I had a certain chemistry. I liked it, always thought of it as our secret show weapon, part of what made us Must See TV.

And here's something I know nobody else knows, not even Alan (because the time was just never right to tell him), Michael and I actually dated, quietly, just a couple times, between the making of the pilot and the series pickup. It was all very PG and by the time the first season wrapped, I was with Alan and Michael and I were just good friends.

Most people don't want to believe that there wasn't more because showmances are so much more fun to speculate on.

"I'm sorry, Alan, if I ever made you unsure about us. I hope you know, I really loved you. Like truly, madly, crazy actress love."

"I know, Kam. Likewise. Best wife I've had so far."

I was number two, of three, so far.

"With the exception of the crying part."

We share a smile on that, because like I said, I cry a lot and to be with me is to just get used it.

"You are going to be okay." Alan puts his hand on me sweetly, then gives a wave, heading off.

I watch him, thinking he's a great guy and then I wonder why is he here on the lot?

"Hey, are you on a show?" I say, brightly, realizing that if Alan is on a show, I could get work.

"I sold a feature, *Naked Ghost Chicks*."

That rings a vague disgust in me. "The one with the ridiculous plot and no real ending?"

"I worked it out. Bella White is directing. We're in prep."

"Wow. Bella's hot right now. That's wonderful, Alan. I'm so happy for you." And I mean it.

And then I go a step too far, literally, walking towards him. "Wasn't there a part in there you wrote for me?"

"Kam…" He says, alarmed by my approach.

"Get me in the room."

"I can't."

"You could."

"I won't."

"You owe…"

"I don't." He cuts me off with a stern, firm look, shakes his head, "It's not gonna happen."

There's a beat where I can tell Alan wants to say something, but is conflicted. He's a nice guy, so I know not to push. It wouldn't go well for me.

He smiles and I think I've made it out without whatever bad thought he was having and then, here it comes, because that is the kind of day I'm having…

"I'm already your rat-bastard ex. You should know what people say about you."

"No, really, Alan. I'm okay not knowing."

"You're not good enough, Kam."

He gives me a look like this is hard for him too. Like in the middle of this I'm supposed to be sorry for him. But I'm not, I can't think beyond the scream of internal pain and anguish breaking out in my head.

"You're a nice southern gal from Georgia. You have a host of amazing skills: You can sing any pop song ever to hit the radio. You make amazing midnight-anything-in-the-cupboard pancakes. You have crazy, mad, good skills in bed. And you're a surprisingly adept Mrs. Goodwrench."

"My dad taught me that…The Goodwrench thing. Not the bed stuff."

I sound so pathetic, which is exactly how I feel. But at least Alan is done, right?

"It's just that, you're not special in this town, babe. There are a hundred girls like you. Most of them younger, prettier, fresher."

I really wish Alan would just wrap up this little overview. I lean against a nearby parked car, breathing steady to keep the panic attack from gripping me further. I'm not good enough. I've heard the rumors, felt the whispers wash over me, hoped it was just my imagination. Sucks to know the truth. I realize Alan is just staring at me, waiting for some response.

I try to make a joke here, "Why we divorced, it's all coming back now." I don't manage the smile at the end that would make that line cute.

"I'm just the messenger here." Alan says, holding up his hands, like you know, this isn't him saying this. "You don't work because you play everything safe. You don't bring it. And until you do, you'll never work in this town again."

EXT. KAMRYN'S HOUSE – POOLSIDE - DAY

My house is a single-level, modern Mediterranean, newish to look old, with a view of the west valley, the flats of Sherman Oaks below and the ocean just over the Santa Monica Mountains. I'm high enough, on a flat lot in the hills, that when the winds shift, I actually get ocean breezes. And most of the year, I get amazing, blazing, yellow, orange summer sunsets. I can't complain.

I like to think I saved this house. It was in a state of disrepair when I bought it on the cheap, and remodeled it on the not-so-cheap.

It was the first of many remodels I would end up doing with show money on summers off, and my favorite, which is why I never turned it over and sold it. It's my own little slice of heaven. All mine: signed, sealed and delivered. Mortgage paid off, compliments of Polly, which is great since…

"My own ex-husband won't hire me. He pretty much said, I'll never work again." I visibly sulk.

I'm poolside, on a chaise, sunglassed and zinced, a towel over my legs to protect me from any offending ray of sun. I'm feeling so low, I gotta reach up to touch the bottom of whatever this pit is I'm wallowing in.

Next to me, on a matching chaise, is my best pal, spiritual guru and certified MFT (Marriage and Family Therapist), DR. ALICIA LUMM, making a house call, in a way only she can.

Lumm is nearly naked in a teensy, tiny bikini which she so has the body to wear. She is 40-something, being quite vague on the something, and fit in a hottie-coed on spring break kind-of-way. Tan and slammin'. And thanks to Pilates, Botox and Collagen, not an extra ounce of fat on her except for those cc's around her lips.

"Don't be blue, sweetie. You've lost your confidence, that's all. That's why you suck at auditions." Lumm swills her drink from a rather oversized martini glass.

"Wow. Thanks for sugar coating that."

"Just get it back. You'll rock again."

"It's not that easy."

When I'm out and about, I usually try and project a cheery, can do appearance. Nobody wants to see a sort-of-famous TV star depressed. But here at home, with Lumm, I can just be me and right now, me is feeling pretty down.

"Yes it is."

She's so full of confidence, it's inspiring. She swings her legs over the chaise and pushes her nearly empty martini glass in my direction.

"Find something you are good at and just do it. Don't let anything or anybody stop you."

"That's it?" I was sort of expecting something more profound.

"That's everything, the secret to success. Dumb, blind, perseverance without a shred of self-consciousness. How do you think Nicole got to where she is?"

Lumm finishes what's in the glass and then seems surprised the glass actually is empty. She holds it up and wiggles it toward my kitchen.

"Yoo who, Consuela? Is it possible to get a little refill out here?"

The double doors are open so there's a straight eye-line into the house.

INT. KAMRYN'S HOUSE – KITCHEN - DAY

CONSUELA GONZALEZ is my ever-present, house-helper. She came to the house one day during construction and just decided she worked there. I can't remember exactly, but I think Consuela might be the wife of one of the tile-layers.

Con could be about 50, but her jet-black hair makes her look years younger. She is short and stout and a fireball of not-to-be-stopped energy. I love her and what she brings to my world, including my super-fluency in all the naughty-bad slang of the Spanish language. When Con drinks, she's got a sailor's mouth and well, she drinks a lot and daily (we're kind of an open bar up here).

She is never dressed in anything but sweat clothes which I'm pretty sure she buys exclusively at Ross Dress

For Less. I think this because she talks constantly of her "es-scores" at Ross.

Apparently they have fantastic deals there. Con's been trying for years to get me to go down the hill with her to one and fight for my clothes off the rack. But honestly, I don't look that great in sweat pants and I'm not really a fight-for-your-deal kind of gal. So I've politely declined each shopping invitation, which always makes her roll her eyes at me.

She finds me and my friends ridiculous for what we spend at places like—well, I won't name them, but they are not places in strip malls in the valley—not that there's anything wrong with that. It's just when you are an actress, people judge what you wear.

Not only do they judge, they take pictures and then shred you publicly online. This happened to me once when I was just having my first brush with fame (I didn't know culottes were 'out') and it so upset me I didn't crawl out of the house for days and then, only after Lumm brought me an entire new outfit from Fred Segal that I felt 'safe' being seen in.

Since then, I'm well, particular about what I wear out. Obsessed might be more accurate.

Con throws Lumm a look and holds her own full martini glass up for Lumm to see and swirls it, just so.

"No. Sorry, missus Alicia. The goose, `ess all gone."

And with that Consuela drinks an entire double martini in one easy motion.

When finished, she gives Lumm a wicked, little smile, then says something in Spanish that might look like

'!?@&*$!' if written out, making it clear who runs this house.

BACK TO SCENE – POOLSIDE

"Well, when the goose's done, so am I." Lumm gets up, throws on her sarong.

"I have scotch." I say, not at all feeling guilty about the possibility of postponing Lumm's 12-step success, which she promises to maybe start, any day now (I'm doubtful).

She teeters just a bit, as she slips on fabulous *Valley of the Dolls* Prada mules.

"I have a house-call session with Iliana and Brad and if I mix, I might just hurl as they babble on about the problems of a two-series couple. Please, some of my clients have real problems, like you."

"Do you forget that I'm sensitive?"

"Oh, Kammikins, man up."

"What kind of spiritual advice is that?"

Lumm pats me on the towel. "That was practical, sweets, and I won't charge for it. I'll make some calls. I must know somebody who can strong-arm Alan..."

"You're the best."

"You are. Believe it. Be it."

She wags her finger then looks away, as if she has forgotten what she was going to say. Then, she turns back to me.

"Stay away from the Fatman."

"Okay. Random. What does that mean?

"No idea. Just came through my head so I thought I'd better say it."

And with that, Lumm sweeps away, leaving me as she always does...

"Remember, reject negativity and..."

"Only possibilities exist," we say together.

We share a smile and a true friendship.

And then with a flourish, she's gone, out the side gate, and I am all alone. Big sigh...

INT. KAMRYN'S DEN – MOMENT LATER

I meander in, pretending to meander, actually, stop for a beat when I see Consuela is here, dusting the shelves full of what she calls, not in the nicest way, La Sustantivo, The Shrine, which is my cherished memorabilia from the show: scripts, props (like my Fedora, my very real looking PI badge, my gun), photo stills and so forth.

Consuela rolls her eyes as I approached the TV remote.

"Ah, missus..." She shakes her head in a sorrowful way.

I don't think it's pathetic to TiVo my show daily. I enjoy watching it. Always have. So, I push past Consuela and inch closer to the wall-mounted flat screen, clicking on the TV and DVR.

As the *My Playlist* unveils itself with nothing but entries of *Polly & Jake, PI*, Consuela tosses me a pathetic look.

"It's been a rough day." I say in my defense as I

choose an episode at random and hit play.

I feel instantly better as my theme music begins to play with the opening credits. You know the kind of sound—jaunty, hummable, with a hint of mystery and danger. Back in the stone ages when my show was in production, series still had long openings, so I get to enjoy essentially a montage of my best, iconic Polly moments. I mime along with the action.

And yes, I know Consuela is rolling her eyes behind me. I don't care. I can remember exactly the show each clip is from and the day we shot them and feel less like a loser just seeing them again.

The credits changed from year to year, but each year always ended with the same scene, a clip from the pilot, the climax, as it was, where I said the words that would become my/Polly's signature line.

I love this part. The villain, Drago, has Polly and is dragging her/me backwards, holding a gun to my/her head.

Polly makes a quick move and flips the villain over, tossing him to the ground, which has the added impossible bonus of knocking the gun from his hand and skittering it far enough away that neither of us can grab at it.

As the villain rolls and recovers, he pops up and comes at me. Surprisingly to him, I am a Jujutsu expert.

We go hand-to-hand in a bit that has the feel of *Crouching Tiger, Hidden Dragon*. I mime along with myself on the TV, marveling how I could move so well in those pants. I remember they were cut so low, I worried about so many things being caught by the camera.

Consuela makes the mistake of trying to cross the room during this fight-along and I do what I often do, involve her.

I put my foot behind her legs, just like Polly is doing on screen and take her down. She lands hard, on her back and makes a face, swearing at me in her usual mutter, resigned to this game.

I stand over her, just as Polly is standing over the villain of the week on the screen, one fist in her face, the other ready to strike.

"Don't you know…" I say along with the TV, "… Polly Parker always gets her man."

The credits end with a MUSIC STING and this week's show begins.

"Just give me warning before you throw me to the floor. That's all I ask."

"You know better than to be in room when I'm Polly." I smile and give her a hand to help her up.

Consuela leans forward, touches her back and looks to me for sympathy. I don't give her any, as I'm now staring at me on the TV, fascinated by my younger self, my so-assuredness.

"I'm good here, aren't I?"

"Yes, missus. You are good as Polly Parker. Very, very good."

Consuela is just being kind, but with such sweetness and conviction. It sends an electric thunderbolt of an idea through me.

EXT. VENICE BEACH - OCEAN FRONT WALK

The tourists, the weirdos, the bikers, the skaters, the usuals do their thing along the bike path. Beyond is sand and ocean. I work out of a rundown, two-story building on the far, north of the path, at the corner, where the street dead ends.

My office is basically a plain, brown-wrapper of a shamus joint...

INT. MICHAEL'S OFFICE - SAME TIME

...Complete with a 40s-style oak chair, desk, and milk-glass interior door with my name stenciled in black paint. Well, mine and my grandfather's. This is the way the place looked when he died and left it to me. I didn't see any reason to redecorate.

There is not a hint of my TV past anywhere here. In fact, there's not a hint of any past. I like it like this. I'm not interested in clients knowing about that part of my life, any part of my past. My past isn't why they come to me. Their past is.

The one redeeming attribute of this office is the view outside my window: sand and ocean, sunshine, most days, with the consistent sound of waves crashing in from the Santa Monica Bay.

The view, the sound, I find, often ease my clients anxieties, so it doesn't surprise me when one of them, such as JOCELYN SWANSON, gets up and moves toward the window.

She told me the first time she came here she was 25, but something in her eyes told me she'd seen more than 25 years could offer.

She's pretty in a Midwest way, which is to say, nobody would look twice at her in LA. It's not that there's anything wrong with her looks, she's just a bit off and a bit thick in a town where the pretty women aren't either of those things.

She did have a figure that she knew how to work a room with. As she approached the window, her back to me, I thought she might be working it now. I didn't mind. I swiveled my chair to follow her movements.

"I got a tip. A source I trust. Your brother is still in town." I say, just to keep sound in the air.

"He's in trouble, isn't it?" She frets while she talks, picking at her gloved hands. She doesn't bother to turn to me, just looks out the window. The evening sunset gives her an interesting glow. Lotsa makeup on this girl. Maybe that's how they do it in the Midwest. What do I know?

"I gotta think that's why you hired me. If there's something you haven't told me yet…"

Jocelyn turns back to me, weighing how much she should reveal.

So far, she's given me very little information to go on, which doesn't bother me, since she's given me a lot of money instead. It's not unusual for my clients to be less than up front with me. What do I care if they want to pay me and then keep me in the dark? I can live with it, as long as it doesn't get me killed.

Just as I think Jocelyn has decided to actually tell me something useful, like maybe why she's really looking for her brother David, there's a commotion in the outer office.

Both Jocelyn and I look to my door as it flies open and in breezes Kamryn in a Fedora. It throws me so completely I swivel in my chair and almost fall out of it.

Jocelyn takes a step back as Kam is closely followed by EFFIE MANETI, my secretary.

"I told you, lady, he's with a client."

"Michael, call off your she-goon." Kam says, as if her blowing in here is a totally normal event in my day.

"Boss, you know this freak?"

All I can do is stare, mouth open. I am suddenly unable to put a few simple words, like "get the hell out of here" together in a sentence.

Why is she wearing a Fedora?

ANOTHER ANGLE – FAVORING KAMRYN

Okay, I tell myself, brave face. Don't let him see you sweat. I turn to the office girl, because I'm half afraid if I turn my back on her, she might jump me. She has that wiry, monkey energy about her.

"I'm Kamryn Cade." I say, expecting her to relax, or maybe gush at having a famous person in the office. But instead, I get zero recognition from her.

I look to Michael who is, well, staring at me, speechless. "You never told her about me?"

There is a weird silence in the room and I sense this is not the big triumphant idea I had imagined in my head driving over here.

"Perhaps I should come back," says the dame, who must obviously be a client.

"No, wait, Ms. Swanson." Michael seems to have suddenly snapped back to reality.

"What're you doing here?" He directs that at me.

"I've come to work a case with you." Obviously.

And then it hits Michael, like a brick. "Is that your stupid hat from the show?"

"It helps me get into character. I have my P.I.'s license too and I even brought my thirty –

"Whoa! Gun! Gun! Everybody down!"

Effie, impressively, pushes Michael out of the way and tries to take me down. But I surprise her with my superior swiftness and karate skills and put her down, hard and fast and stand over her, one fist in her face, the other ready to strike.

"Hi!" I yell. And then for emphasis: "Ha."

"Wow. Where did you learn that?"

"Episode one-dash-seven, *Case of the Jade Panda.* I went undercover in the Yakuza."

The client seems uncertain, looks to Michael.

"You've lost your mind."

I help Effie up. "Nope. I'm totally clear. This is what I do well. Being a detective is what I'm good at."

"You're not a detective. You never were."

"I have five years experience. I've solved ninety-seven cases."

"That's very impressive," says client lady. She smiles at me.

"I know. Kamryn Cade. You may have heard of me." I say, reaching out to shake her hand.

"No." Client lady does not offer her hand to mine. In fact, she curls her hand towards her chest, clutching, almost. I notice that her brocade top is quite elegant, but not appropriate for a girl her age. Weird choice.

I turn to look at the office girl, who clearly is wondering who I am as well.

"You don't know me?"

"Should I?" She really doesn't seem to.

"Doesn't anybody here watch TV?"

Both the client and the office girl shake their heads, and then…

"Wait a minute…" And I can see recognition in the dark-haired, cubicle dweller… "You're that actress who was on that…" And then she looks to Michael, a light going off. "*YOU* were Mr. Stubbled, Hollywood-hunk, fake-detective, sidekick guy?"

I look away. That is a road kill description and I know Michael will not be pleased.

"I'm a real detective, Effie, was before the show, still am now." He sort of whispers this through clenched teeth.

"You didn't know?" I say, incredulously to Effie.

"I'm new and he doesn't really tell me much."

"He can be like that." I nod, knowing. Michael is such a withholder.

I'm taken totally by surprise as he suddenly grabs my arm, yanking me to follow him out the door.

As soon as I've cleared it, he slams it closed, which, unfortunately, the top part, made of glass, breaks and shatters, revealing Effie and Jocelyn watching us like a Mexican soap opera.

"I reject your negativity," I say, proactively.

"You need to wait until I actually say something."

"You were about to. And I know it's not going to be nice. So, I only want to see possibilities."

"Of what, getting your ass kicked out the front door?"

The ancient, black, dial phone on the front desk RINGS and RINGS, a good, LOUD, old-fashioned RING. Nobody moves to get it.

"Effie!"

She answers the phone on Michael's desk. We watch her through the broken door pane.

"Barlowe Investigations. Hold one second, Mr. Swanson."

Effie gives Michael a look. "Him."

Michael picks up the outer-office phone.

"Barlowe... Yeah. Okay. Name the place."

Michael scribbles on a piece of paper, shoves it in his pocket and then hangs up, looks to Jocelyn, who's come out of his office to join us in the front area.

"He heard I'm looking for him, wants to meet."

"I want to go," coos the client.

"So do I." I blurt out without thinking how inappropriate this might be.

Michael ignores me, turns this attention to Ms. Swanson.

"I'll handle this. Go back to your hotel. I'll call you."

Jocelyn nods and he walks her to the front office door.

She gives him a sultry look, touches him on the forearm, "If David's scared... Well, be careful, Mr. Barlowe."

Michael nods and then she exits. He turns to me and glares. Effie comes out to her desk and watches us.

"So what's her story? Who's David? Lost Lover? Some Joe who's done her wrong? Two-timing boyfriend, what?" I think if I can get him to tell me, I'm in.

"He's her..." Effie starts, but then...

"Close your trap, Effie."

"But if I'm working the case..." Still trying...

.   Michael crosses to Effie's desk and starts to ransack the drawers, clearly looking for something.

"I don't know what you're going through, Kam, and I don't in any way care.

"You are so not nice these days."

"I'm not in the nice business anymore."

He turns around, handcuffs in his hands and slaps a cuff on me, rough and fast.

"Why do I get the feeling you've done that before?"

He pulls me over to a heavy metal chair, forces me down with a powerful shove.

"Aw, c'mon. I won't follow you."

"That's right, not now. But you were going to because that's what Polly would do."

He tosses the keys to Effie.

"Give me ten, then put her out on her ass."

Effie nods. He heads out, slamming the front office door, which unfortunately, also has a top panel made of milk glass. It shatters. He gives me the evil eye.

"You can hardly blame me for that."

But it's pretty clear he does.

INT. MICHAEL'S CAR – NIGHT

Elysian Park is Los Angeles' oldest public park. It's mostly trees and trails, but also boasts your standard assorted smattering of public buildings, playground areas and groomed picnic grounds. It also encompasses Chavez Ravine, where Dodger Stadium and the Police Academy are located.

Most people have seen pictures of it because parts of the park, just east of downtown, are high enough to have a postcard view of the city skyline. It's a standard in a lot of films, looks especially impressive at night.

Maybe that's why David, the guy I'm after, who supposedly has only been in town a couple of weeks, wants to meet here, of all places, and late, when it's closed. He's a movie fan. Who knows? Maybe he thinks it's safe, unaware that at night it's heavily populated by the homeless, the Hispanic gangs, the meth/crack heads, the prostitutes and the foolish lovebirds who take their lives into their own hands by coming here for a quickie with a view.

The murder/robbery count in this park is often and daily. Not that that bothers me. It's not the danger of the place I mind so much, but the fact that to get here, I had to spend an hour on the 10 freeway during rush-hour traffic. I would have preferred a neutral meeting someplace closer to the Westside, but it wasn't offered to me and since I've been chasing this guy for a week now, I just want to get in front of him and see what the deal is between him and my client.

At least the crawl across town gave me some time to cool down about the Kam thing. She is clearly having some sort of meltdown, worse than just her usual crying jags, which, after a while, you kind of get used to. I might enjoy watching it if I didn't happen to have this front row seat. Work a case with me? Her career must really be in the dump.

As I come near the turn off to the Simons Lodge, where, in theory, David should be waiting for me, I shut my lights off and pull the car to the side of the road, just after the turn, parking behind some brush. It's not perfect, but at night, hidden enough somebody heading down to the lodge after me should miss it.

I sit a minute in the quiet of the night and listen. The sound of nothing is comforting. I have never liked the scratchings and noises of nature. This park, I remember now, also has a mountain lion warning in effect. I decide to take my gun out of the glove box, as much for the mountain lion as anybody I might meet along the way.

EXT. ELYSIAN PARK – NIGHT

I suppose a trusting person would walk down the road and right up to the lodge gate and simply wait for a dangerous stranger to arrive. I'm not that person.

I double back up the paved road to where I can see the main lodge below. There is a low-watt utility light so I can see the surrounding area clear enough to get a sense of the set up.

There are two covered pavilions for outdoor events, some benches near a pond, and a cascading water feature. In the middle of the water feature is a wooden bridge, which is where I'm supposed to wait for David. I scan the surroundings and can't see any movement. It's possible I'm the first one here.

I edge quietly down the dirt trail on the side of the road, until I come to...

EXT. SIMONS LODGE – ENTRANCE AREA

There is only one way in to the lodge's pavilion, a set of iron gates, which are perpetually simply left open. I move down the path and take up a vantage point, about fifty feet from the gates, behind some hedges and hunker down for the wait. It's dark here and there are more of those noises and scratches of nature than I'd like.

I'm so focused on scanning the darkness of the parking lot area and the entry gates that I don't at first notice that the TWIG SNAPPING noise behind me is very close. I slip behind a large palm and as the person who is coming towards me from behind is close enough, I grab them, placing my hand over their mouth and pulling them down behind my hedge, fist up to land a shot, until I see…

"Kam? What the? How did you find me?"

ANOTHER ANGLE – FEATURING KAMRYN

I mumble through Michael's hand, which is still on my mouth. He removes it, but indicates for me to be quiet, so I whisper.

"I have my ways, darling." I say in spot on Russian. "You will have to kill me before I tell you."

I smile, but Michael just stares at me. It's obvious he doesn't get it at all.

"Natasha…" I say in English now. Yeah, still nothing. "The episode where I joined the KGB."

"This isn't a game. I've been after this guy and he's been impossible to pin down. Don't mess this…"

There is another really loud TWIG SNAP. Michael shushes me and makes a move to get into position. Suddenly, a heavy set figure is before him. Michael jumps them and wrestles them to the ground. I know this is a mistake and tap him repeatedly with one finger on his back to get him to stop.

"Wait, wait." I whisper.

Michael stops, looks at me, then at the person on the ground. "I know you. You're her maid."

Consuela sits up, dusting dirt from her sweat outfit. "House-helper."

"I told you to wait by the cars."

"I got es-scared."

"You had your may... house-helper tail me?"

"A good detective always has a backup plan."

"You're not a good detective."

"I had the back-up plan, didn't I?"

Another BRANCH CRACKLE. Michael shoos the women back a step and then jumps the next person. He tackles them, takes them to the ground and rolls them over.

The women rush forward to see who it is. It's a sweet-faced, college kid, skinny, bespectacled, fiercely geeky.

"Who is this, your pool-helper?"

I shrug. No idea.

"I'm MILO FARNSWORTH, sir. I'm so excited to meet you and Ms. Cade."

"You are?" I say, liking him immediately, helping him up.

"I'm your biggest fan. I've loved your show ever since I was a kid. I'm a UCLA FILM/TV major now, doing my thesis on TV detective duos: sexual tension and crime solving as a paradigm of man's quest for love in the modern world."

"That's sad, kid."

"Michael..." I swat at him and then turn to Milo "It's not, Milo. That sounds very interesting."

"I've been following you, Ms. Cade, hoping I could

get an interview with, well, both of you.

"No."

"Of course."

Michael and I overlap in our totally opposite replies.

"How about later? We're on a case now."

"Awesome. Do you mind if I..."

Another NOISE, Michael and Kam both place a hand over Milo's mouth at the same time.

Kam throws a look to Michael. "You want me to take this one?"

Michael shakes his head, gets ready for the next guest, who turns out to be...

"Jocelyn?"

"I just want to see my brother."

"Why?" I jump forward, get into her space. "What's he done? Or are you trying to stop him from doing something? Come on, little sister, talk to me."

She takes a step back, away from me.

"Kam. Shut up." Michael seems to be protective of her. I don't much like it.

ANGRY VOICES from the darkened parking lot pierce the night and then, THREE GUN BLASTS.

"Stay put." Michael takes off running, towards the sound of gunfire. I find that sort of brave and inspiring...

EXT. PARK - PARKING LOT - NIGHT

Michael flies into the empty lot and stops when he sees a man's dead body under a pool of light at the far end of the lot. I, Consuela, Milo and Jocelyn bump into him as we were running fast, right behind him.

A car in the distance, SQUEALS OFF, drives over a dirt curb and disappears into the dark of night. No way to chase it. No way to see the plate.

Milo approaches the body and rolls the man over.

Jocelyn edges up, fearfully. "Oh, thank God. He's not David."

I stare, I'll admit, somewhat fascinated. I've never seen a real, dead person. I have to say, they look a lot like the fake dead people on any given set, except, of course, there will be no 'cut' to give them reprieve.

Sad, I think. Whoever this guy is, he is somebody's family. "We should do something to help him," I say to no one in particular.

Michael throws me a look. "He's dead, Kam. It's a little late for that."

Milo expertly rifles the pockets of the man. "No I.D."

I am distracted by cigarette butts left on the ground near where the body fell, irritated actually. I bend down to pick them up. "How hard is it to just put these in the trash? Really gets me how smokers think it's okay to just–Ow! Still hot."

Michael picks up a butt, smells it, examines it.

"Does David smoke?"

"Sometimes."

Michael then gives me a look. "Nice idea to toss out the evidence."

'I'm rusty. I still have this, though."

I'm holding a matchbook that I picked up right before the hot, smoking butt (that's just fun to say).

Milo comes up next to me, peers at the evidence like it's a golden ticket, "La Viva Diablo."

"Ah, the Devil lives. Ess a bad sign." Consuela is unnerved by this matchbook, looks around, worriedly.

"It's a nightclub. In downtown. Not a sign the devil is coming for us…"

But Consuela is unconvinced by my matter-of-fact attitude, shakes her head at me and I think curses me softly under her breath. She drops to her knees and begins a fervent prayer in hushed Spanish. Jocelyn and Michael throw a look at her and then to me.

"She's devout." I give a shrug. Not the first time I've seen that and besides, when has a little prayer not been a good thing?

"How do you know it's downtown?" Michael is at my side, trying to take the matchbook from my hand.

"It says so. 323 Palmetto Street." I say, feeling somewhat the smartie pants, sort of moving the pack in a way that he can't snatch it… easily.

He grabs my hand, hard, and then removes the matchbook from it. I let him have it, whatever.

He reads it, pockets it. "We should call the police," is his only reaction.

"Right." I say, pulling out my cell.

Milo holds his phone. "Hey, wow, we have the same phone. Cool beans."

It's an iPhone, so millions of people have them, but it's still pretty cute that he gets a charge out of this.

"I'll do it." Milo says, as he's already dialing.

I look over to see that Michael has moved to the middle of the parking lot and is speaking to his client privately. Consuela is still on her knees, praying.

Jocelyn, I can see, might be a little freaked out by all of us. She keeps looking past Michael at Consuela and then over to me. I simply smile as Milo fills the 911 operator in on our parking-lot murder with surprisingly good details about time and where we are and how to find us.

I move a step or two away from the pack, looking at the night sky. I know a man is lying dead at my feet and all that, but the LA sky can be really amazing sometimes, weirdly dark and bright all at once. And the quiet of the park is lovely. I drift back a step, closer to the wooded area at the edge of the lot, gazing up, loving the wonder of it all.

Suddenly Michael is next to me, pulling me back towards him, away from the woods, in an action that feels like something we've done a million times before. And then it hits me, it's his I'm-saving-you-from-danger move.

He slides between me and the dark edge as I turn to look and find I am a mere few feet away from a MYSTERIOUS CHINESE MAN who is standing quietly, watching, smoking, holding a shiny, long-barreled gun on me, probably a classic .9mm toggle-lock action Luger, if I had to guess.

He looks from me to Michael, kind of hard to read his blank face. Michael and I stand very still. Milo, Jocelyn and Consuela freeze where they are. And all is deathly quiet.

Michael holds his hands up. Not going to do anything too fast, or too forward.

The Mysterious Chinese Man steps toward us, to Michael, pressing his gun against Michael's chest.

Michael moves just slightly so that he is now squarely between me and the Mysterious Chinese Man. I can feel him breathe deeply, steadily. He doesn't look away. He holds the gaze of the man as the man reaches into Michael's waistband and takes Michael's gun.

He flicks Michael's gun back and forth and we take it to mean he wants us to step back, so we do. We all fall back into one group, staring at the silent man.

He drags deeply on his cigarette, the butt glowing hot orange in the night. He looks at us, the body on the ground, as if he'd like to get closer. But he is stopped by the flashing blue lights coming over the park hill.

In one quick move, he tosses Michael's gun across the parking lot. It skitters away, from the light into dark, so that we can only follow it by the sound of metal skipping over asphalt.

For some reason, I turn to watch where the gun will land. Not sure why. And as I turn back to see where the Mysterious Chinese Man is, I'm surprised to find he's gone, disappeared into the inky black of the park.

I'm about to say something, my usual something, whatever that might be in this kind of circumstance, but I stop. I realize Michael is trembling, a little bit, just his hand, the one nearest me, as he keeps an eye on the space where the mysterious man disappeared into.

I instinctively take his hand. Surprisingly, he lets me. He turns to me and I smile. It's a moment he doesn't hate me.

"Jesus, Kam. Way to almost get me killed." He pulls away and we're back.

The blue flashing lights descend upon us.

FADE OUT.

END ACT ONE

ACT TWO

FADE IN:

EXT. PARK PARKING LOT – LATER

Part of the job I hate: dealing with cops. So many of them in LA are straight up sociopaths, attracted to the job for the power and gun and the knowledge that, on any given night, they might be able to shoot somebody with impunity. This isn't your small town police department here to help. When they say "...to Protect and to Serve," they generally mean themselves. If they actually help the rest of us in the course of that pursuit, well, that's just a side thing.

Within minutes of the first squad coming over the hill, the parking lot was lousy with them: uniforms, detectives, administrators, crime scene photogs, the body-carters and a whole crowd of no-idea-what-their-purpose-is kind of bureaucrats. LAPD sent an army of twenty or so to mop up after one dead body. For a city that's got any number of dead bodies every night, it's not a mystery why the department's broke. *CYA (cover your...)* management costs a bundle.

Cops hate private detectives right back, equally. We tend to crash their parties and unrestrained by paperwork and procedure, muck up their world, like tonight.

They were not amused to learn, that before they got here, we'd already rolled the body, searched it and chased off what could possibly an actual eyewitness.

Tainted was a word being whispered from cop to cop as they threw lousy looks towards our motley pack: The shady detective, the oddly-mannered, Midwest client, the perky actress, the devout, fervent, foul-mouthed Hispanic maid in sweatpants and the kid. Jesus, how did my case go so far wrong, so fast?

I look toward Kam, who's at my side... She's actually smiling at every cop, enjoying the production value of the murder scene. If we weren't surrounded by twenty badges, I might actually strangle her on the spot.

I am straight up in a profoundly bad mood, which is why I'm actually glad it's OFFICER GINA D'AMICO who grabs the assignment to interview us: me, Kam and the maid (the kid was whisked away by a plain-clothes detective and my client has drifted to the edge of the lot with no one paying much attention to her).

I know D'Amico from around. She, at least, I can stand to have a conversation with. And she's not half-bad to look at either. Long hair, I'm betting (if it were down), dark and she's got exotic in her somewhere, just enough to explain the hint of Mediterranean skin. No telling where the green eyes come from. It's a good mix, though. Out of the uniform, she's probably show-stopping, every bit as much as Kam. She must've grown up with brothers. She seems totally comfortable with men–no need to put on a show. I like that. She makes the questioning bearable. And, it turns out, who knew, she's got a sense of humor about her work. She is clearly amused, unfortunately, at my expense.

"So, you cuff the actress, which sounds like a certain kind of fun… Then drive out here, Mr. Master Detective, not realizing Miss Cade's operative was tailing you?"

"She's not an operative. She's…"

She cuts me off, "I know. I have it right here. House-helper."

"I think maid is very demeaning." Kam interjects, thinking the world always wants to know what she's thinking at the moment she's thinking it. "Not that there's anything wrong with being a maid. The term is just so limiting."

Consuela nods. "I do many things, not just clean."

D'Amico looks from the girls to me. I throw up my hands. I mean, really, I could care less. I just want this Kam-induced nightmare to end.

D'Amico stays in professional mode. "Right. Okay. That seems fair." She jots something in her notebook.

"I think so too." Consuela says to Kam.

"I try to treat you right."

"I so appreciate that in you. You are a good boss."

Kam, touched by Consuela's words, hugs her. D'Amico looks at me again, like, really? "Are these new employees of your firm?"

"No." I assure her. And then to my shock I hear…

"Yes." Kam says as she comes out of the hug with Consuela.

"No." I say as if talking to a child with special needs.

She turns to D'Amico, "It's complicated."

Officer D'Amico looks from Kam to me.

"It's not." I mean, really what more do I have to say to get this through to her?

Kam just looks at me, all wide-eyed, vulnerable and beautiful. That's her trick look, been a long time since I've fallen for that. I stare back, not giving an inch.

She gives first, turns to D'Amico. "He's right. It's not…"

Okay, good. I got through to her (finally).

"You see, I've found something I'm good at and I'm going to do it. And I'm not going to let anyone tell me I can't. Especially not him." Kam nods defiantly towards me.

"Well, good for you." D'Amico seems genuinely feeling the moment of girl power.

"Exactly. You so get it, don't you?"

D'Amico smiles "I'm trying."

She steers back to business. "So, the somebody yelling, what do you think that was all about?"

A squad car pulls up next to us and OFFICER DROBEK, a fifty-something old-timer, worn-out, rumpled cop-type gets out. He's carrying a Starbuck's cup.

"Excuse me, Ms. Cade…"

D'Amico lowers her notebook, not pleased. "Drobek. I'm working here."

"I don't want her chai latte to get cold." He says, with a genuine shrug. He hands the cup to Kam.

"Thank you so much, Officer. You positively define LA's finest."

The schmuck cop glows. D'Amico simply cannot believe the effect Kam is having on her co-worker.

"Are you the officer whose daughter loves my, I mean, *our* show? Michael, of course, was my co-star."

D'Amico shoots me a look. Subtle, belated recognition mixed with more amusement.

Schmuck cop doesn't even glance my way. He's just so in awe of Kam. "Yes, ma'am. She never misses it. Runs every night on DTV."

"I know. I don't miss it either. I TiVo it." Kam smiles to him, as if she's sharing a secret with a special friend and then touches him sweetly.

This is her I'm down with the little people act. Which she seems always so sincere about. Like she actually likes these people. It kills me. It always works. Everybody loves her, except, I guess, me.

I look at D'Amico. She, at least, doesn't seem to be falling over herself in the presence of a half-baked, once-upon-a-freaking-long-time-ago TV star. And she TiVo's reruns? I've never even watched a full episode since the pilot. I could never stand to see what I had done to myself.

"Would you like me to sign something for her?" Kam says, leading Officer Drobek away.

"I sure would. She'll be so thrilled."

The two of them walk off. "Buenas noches, Consuela. Manana."

"Thank you, Missus Kam, nos de Dios." And with that, Consuela heads out.

D'Amico and I watch as Kam works the murder scene like she's the star of this set. "Milo, as my official biggest fan, do you have a photo of me in your car?"

"I do." Milo says, only too happy to be of help to Kam. "I'll go get it."

The officer interviewing Milo indicates his squad car. "Hop in, kid. I'll ride you up there."

And like that, Kam has cleared the area.

D'Amico closes her notebook, dumbfounded. "She just stole my show."

"Welcome to the club."

"That was you two? Polly and Jake?"

"Don't start with me, Gina."

She smiles at me, taps her notebook on her hand. A nervous habit maybe. Do I make her nervous? That's an interesting thought.

"I knew you had something like that in your past. You know, people talk. But to see you two together, it's kind of freaky."

"You have no idea. Like I've slid into some alternate universe."

"Nah. That's another show." She smiles warmly.

"I don't want to be in that one either."

Another officer approaches us and hands D'Amico an evidence bag with my gun in it. She opens the bag and sniffs, then eyes me.

"Clearly not fired. But you know, we gotta log it in, run the tests. I'll get it back to you soonest."

"Thanks."

Office D'Amico heads off. I look over to Kam, who's

now surrounded by an adoring pack of LA's boys in blue (could be some femcops too, hard to tell sometimes). She's signing notebooks for them. They're lining up for pictures with her. Amazing how perfectly sane people freak out over the famous.

ANOTHER ANGLE – ON KAM

The police in LA are just the greatest. So friendly and helpful. They do an amazing job in a tough city.

I adore them, totally, and I'm pretty thrilled that they seem to adore me (Polly) as well. Nothing wrong with being surrounded by men in uniform. I love men in uniform: cops, ballplayers, our brave men in the military, oh and, firemen... Firemen especially, a lifelong weakness.

In every ear is some sweet voice telling me how much they enjoy my show. Some days a girl just needs this sort of thing. I smile with genuine happiness as pictures here and there are snapped of me and the boys.

I notice Michael heading off with Jocelyn, whom, I have decided, I don't much like, mostly because I don't get a sense she likes me. Either that or it's because I'm pretty sure she's lying about, well, almost everything. I can't prove it (yet), but I'll see how it plays out.

I excuse myself from my boys in blue and cross to intersect Michael and Ms. Swanson before they hit the path that leads out the parking lot and back up the hill.

"What's up? Where are you going?"

"I'm tired. Michael is going to take me back to my hotel." Jocelyn feigns an exhausted fragileness.

"I just, one second…" And I grab Michael and pull him a few steps away.

"You can't go. We have a lot to talk about. What do you want me to do? What's our next move?"

"*We* don't have a next move." Michael, is always so edgy with me. I try not to take it personally.

"What about La Viva Diablo? Shouldn't we stake that out? What about I.D-ing the vic? What's the…"

"Stop the Nancy Drewing." Michael hisses at me. "You're a menace. You could have gotten killed tonight, or worse, you could have gotten *me* killed. And there's a high probability that man we found is dead because of you. He'd probably be alive if you didn't have this pathological need to constantly pretend to be somebody you're not."

Jocelyn, not far enough away, has heard this all, looks at me with a pathetic sympathy.

"You don't have to be so cruel all the time."

"Apparently I do, because nothing else seems to get through to you. Your hare-brain makes you dangerous."

"You jerk. I am not hare-brained. I happen to have a very high I.Q.: Mensa high."

"Yeah," he snarks. "That must be why you're an actress."

"Oh, I see. If I were truly smart, I'd be something else? Something stable: an ad exec, a banker, maybe a lawyer? Then for the rest of my life, I'd be stuck doing one thing and one thing only?"

"That's what a normal person does."

"I'm normal." I say, getting irked with him.

"In what universe?"

"This one." I say, arms out, indicating here, now. "Being only one thing in life would kill me. I'd be bored out of my mind. I need more and acting gives me that. I've been an ad exec, a banker, a laywer—four times, thank you very much. I've also been an Olympic gymnast, a nuclear scientist, a time-traveler, a Russian spy, an astronaut..."

I'm really starting to ramp this up, when suddenly behind me, I hear:

"A trapeze artist!"

I turn to find my pack of adoring police has drifted near to Michael and me. They have come to cheer me on and support me (told you, I love them).

"Right. A hooker, a gold rush girl..." I go on.

"A race car driver!" yells Officer Drobek. "I just saw it the other day."

"A..."

Michael cuts me off. "Okay. I get it."

"I don't think you do. I've learned more in those roles than most people learn in a lifetime. And I love every minute of every day I get to go to work. So don't you for a moment stand there and think me stupid for doing what I love."

For good measure, I stomp my foot. And as I do, the crowd erupts in APPLAUSE. Even Officer D'Amico is clapping for me.

I do a little bow to the crowd. "Thank you. Now, if

we could just have a little privacy. We need to discuss our case."

The crowd disperses. I smile at Michael. "So, am I in?"

"No."

Oooh, that Michael.

He turns to go and I need to think fast. I need to get to him, need something to turn this my way. Desperate, I do something I know isn't very nice.

"This is about your ego, isn't it? You're afraid I'll be better than you. Again. It's one thing for the actress to out act you. Quite another for the actress to out detect you."

"Careful, Kam," he seethes. At least I know I've hit him low enough to get his attention.

"Or what?" I stand my ground, unafraid. What's the worst Michael could do, turn his back on me, walk away, never talk to me again? Yeah, been there, done that.

"You two are interesting." Jocelyn watches us, not quite sure what to make of what she's seen today (frankly, neither am I).

"What is it you want from me?"

"A chance." I mean it. That's what I want in life. "And, well, an opportunity to show you I'm good, some fun and to help people. Yeah. Those are the things I want."

And then, another light-bulb idea hits me (been a really creative day): "Tell you what, I crack this case, we partner up. You solve it. I go away, never to bother you again."

"That's insane."

I can tell Michael can't quite compute the idea. He's

a Taurus. They don't pivot that fast.

"You are not a real detective. You weren't even that good of a fake detective," he stammers, looking for any good reason to keep me at bay.

"C'mon, Michael. Think outside your little box. I can be a huge asset to you, your agency."

"I look at you, Kam, and I'll see is a big, red check in the liabilities column. Besides, I have a client to think about."

"You mean, hide behind?" Might as well go all in on this, nothing to lose now. "Ms. Swanson, would you mind if I worked on your case? No extra charge."

Michael's jaw drops. He really didn't see that coming. Or this:

"I think that would be fine, if it's okay with Mr. Barlowe."

A beat. Michael looks between his two problems. I can see him calculating: What is his best play here, …if any?

He grabs my arm, drags me a few feet away, not gently. When we get far enough from the client, he burns that laser death stare at me again.

"You promise, right here, when I solve this, you crawl back under that Hollywood sign and never bother me again."

I smile. I got him. He's game. "Yes. You solve it first. I'm gone. I solve it, I'm moving into Barlowe Investigations. I noticed a small office next to yours not being used."

"That's the storage closet," he snarls.

"Well see…" I snarl right back.

Oh, the look in his eyes: wide, whites showing fear.

He tosses me another foot forward (just because he can, I guess), pulls a picture out of his pocket, shoves it toward my face.

"David Swanson. He just spent two years in prison for drug charges, petty stuff. He's supposedly gone clean, but his P.O. can't find him. I hear from the street, he's working one last, big score. La Viva Diablo is a gang-run nightclub downtown. Dicey place, owned by a guy named Ramon. He doesn't like the way you look, he might just ice you. Now you know as much as I do."

He shoves the picture back into his pocket.

"How do you know about that guy and the club?"

"Jocelyn. She says David's been trying to meet Ramon."

"So, she's not been telling you everything."

Michael laughs. "My clients never tell me everything. Nature of the job. They all lie until the bodies start falling. And even then, they just tell you whatever little they think they can get away with. You just gotta hope that none of the bodies that fall are yours."

"I'm not going to scare off that easily." I say, thinking Michael is trying to inject a sense of uh-oh into this gambit.

"It's not a game, Kam. You gotta know that."

I nod. "Contrary to what you think, Michael, I can handle reality."

"Ha!" He scoffs at me.

"Okay, look. My turn here. Listen up: My instincts tell me our client is a liar. Not sure yet about what, but my guess is the wounded little sister act. She's been flirting with you, so I'm sure you haven't noticed, but a real worried sister would be thinking about her brother. That would stifle any sexual thoughts. She's not stifling. My guess is, this David guy, she used to sleep with him. And why is she always fiddling with her hands? Something about her isn't quite right, which makes her dangerous to both of us. Now you know as much as I do."

A beat. Michael eyes Jocelyn, nods.

"Shake on it, partner?"

I offer my hand to him for a good, solid, bet of our lifetime handshake.

He takes my tiny hand and grips it hard and long and strong. We share a weirdly electric (and awesome) look. It fills me with a little cockiness.

"Throw in your office?" I dare him. "I like the view there."

His eyes narrow and then he matches me with: "Sure. Throw in your car."

I'm totally caught off-guard. "My Mercedes? That's my baby…"

"Where's your confidence, Kam?"

He's hit me at a weak place, that confidence thing everybody keeps talking about. But I hate anybody knowing I have a weakness, don't even like the idea of that notion out there in the ether, taking root. So I muster my old friend, *Bravado*.

"Fine. But when I solve this first, the stencil on the door is going to read: Cade & Barlowe."

Michael actually grunts and tightens his jaw, but shakes my hand one last time.

As he turns to walk off, he turns back: "You get

killed, it's not on me."

And with that, he's off to rejoin his/our client.

I watch them move out, up the hill and then do a little victory dance.

I'm on a case… I'm on a case. And it's for real. Wow. Now what?

FADE OUT.

<u>END ACT TWO</u>

ACT THREE

FADE IN:

EXT. WARNER BROS. STUDIOS – BACKLOT

It's late afternoon and even though the sun is still high in the valley sky, a chill of a wind from the coast actually ekes its way through the Barham Pass and onto the lot.

I love walking on this lot, any lot, and get a kick out of watching whatever is being set up for or actually being shot.

Contrary to what one might think, crews rarely shoo looky-loos away. You get so used to people watching everything you do (I mean, isn't that kind of the point of our business?), you never mind when they actually stop to take a look.

I'm crossing what is called New York Street right now, a row of brownstones, or well, the façades of brownstones. There aren't really any rooms behind the fronts of the buildings, not rooms you'd shoot anything in, just boxes of lumber, really, enough of a place you could shoot somebody coming out of the building, or looking out the window. If you needed an interior scene, you'd have to move to a stage for that.

The crew here is wrapping whatever shoot they did today. The company (the crew, director, actors, everybody) is gone, probably filming on a nearby stage. Those left behind to wrap are the lower key personnel who always get stuck with the clean-up duty. It sounds like a bummer and in some ways can be. But we all know it's an apprentice town.

If you are not Hollywood royalty (related to a big exec or major above-the-line personnel: director, producer, writer, actor/actress) you are expected to work your way up through the ranks.

Some day these clean up peeps will be the keys–running the show. Knowing that makes all the lower rung stuff that much more bearable.

I look over the set dec (pronounced 'set deck.' This is all the props and decorations in a scene): fake snow on the ground, holiday decorations. A Christmas shoot in April.

By the time they post and digitally add breath to each actor's exhales, you will swear to your mother this scene was shot on location in New York in the dead of an East Coast winter. I tell you, it's magic what we do in Hollywood and if you let yourself embrace it, it can be wonderful.

I turn off the street and find all the production vehicles parked behind the brownstone façade structure, which, if you have never seen the back of a façade, resembles abandoned construction, half-built and left to dry out and rot over the years.

I'm sure it's safe. The studios are crazy-concerned about making every part of the magic process super-safe, but one wonders if OSHA wandered by if they wouldn't be tempted to red tag some of these sets just on principle.

At the end of the trailer-fest that comes with every production, is a plain, long, silver hauler: The Key Wardrobe trailer (where the good stuff is kept). I get a thrill just at the sight of it. I love wardrobe and more importantly, I love this particular wardrobe-wizard like no other. I knock on the door.

The door is opened by a 50'ish balding, pudgy man wearing a multi-colored Nehru jacket and breath-defying pencil-leg skinny pants, in velvet. This is STAN-DARLING. You can always spot the wardrobe team on set. They always look fabulous, with an intrinsic sense of flair and grooviness that is just, well, impressive.

Stan-Darling gives me a look up and down and then frowns at me. "Why do you insist on wearing a sack every-where? You are a perfect size two. You shouldn't hide it."

As per my usual mode, I am in some cut and color of a down this or that. When you are small, like I am, you don't carry a lot of fat to keep you warm. So I compensate my personal deficiency with duck feathers. Right now, it's a three-quarter length, tight-weave, grey parka. "I'm not hiding it. Just keeping it warm."

We share smiles and hugs.

"For a certain somebody I hope." Stan-Darling gives

me a sympathetic look.

"Just little ole me." I say, encouraging more pity.

He sighs. "Such a waste."

He takes me by the hand and moves me about like a doll he's thinking of changing costumes on (which he is).

Stan-Darling was, of course, my wardrobe guru on *Polly & Jake*. Over the course of those five years, we spent many hours in and out of clothes, laughing, joking, doing and wearing the most ridiculous things, just for fun.

You become unbelievably close when you do a series (so many hours spent together). I may miss him the most of the many great people I worked with.

I knew, when this new idea, *this case*, became real, I would need to get some of my Polly back and that first step rests with Stan.

"Okay, sweetie. Who do you need to be?"

He and I share a look, an understanding, a kinship. Costumes are fun.

EXT. LA VIVA DIABLO CLUB – NIGHT

Downtown, but not the good section. It's a couple blocks just shy of produce row, meaning close to the river wash and nearby to nothing. There's no line of sexy wannabe starlets here, no crowd willing to endure humiliation to get in.

I've been standing down the block watching the place for fifteen minutes. Nothing is happening. I don't know why sometimes I do this stand-and-watch thing, but I guess it gives me some illusion of controlling the environment of the case.

But who am I kidding? My case is spiraling towards disaster like I'm partnered with the Tasmanian Devil... This thought makes me almost smile. I am. Kam.

I keep thinking about how she railroaded me into this bet thing. Why does she have this power that makes me do the stupid? I had better solve this thing and fast, like lightning, or I just know, I'm going to be a sorry man. Hell, I'm sorry already.

If only I had not agreed to the B! interview for losers thing.

My track record on making all the wrong choices just grows longer. When this is done, I gotta make some changes, because my life is just moving down a bad, dark alley. But that's work for another day. I guess it's about time I sucked up this night and got into the swamp.

INT. LA VIVA DIABLO – MOMENT LATER

As soon as I open the door to the joint, two things hit me: The sound and the smell. One is pleasant, the other will probably make me high and possibly nauseous if I spend too much time wallowing in this hole.

The hip thing for these thugs (and that's what these young kids are today) are called *blunts*, cheap cigars hollowed out and stuffed with whatever Maui-wowee they're peddling in this decade. I wouldn't know. I'm not cool and I don't partake.

I've never understood the appeal of being high, which for me was really just low and intensely paranoid. But I guess, you know, to each their own, whatever floats your boat. Nobody judges. Too bad. Some of these boys could use some swift judgment in the behind. Then maybe they wouldn't be sitting here puffing their futures away.

As I cross the club and head for the bar, I glance at the lounge singer. You kind of have to. She's something. Classy, comes to mind and so does out-of-place.

She's crooning real slow and sexy and while I don't do Spanish, her meaning is clear. I am puzzled though at her get-up. The dress is clingy and low cut and a ten in my book, but then on her head is some kind of fruit basket thing that makes me think of the name Carmen Miranda.

Carmen, as I recall from the old, weirdly-exuberant, MGM musicals, was a lounge singer of some note and she was, in fact, famous for her turban headdresses of colorful things, including fruit. But you kind of have to be old to know about her and the girl on stage, from the look of her figure, she's too young for that. Weird choice, but maybe turbans of fruit are making a comeback. I have long ago stopped trying to stay current with pop culture. Frankly, I don't give a damn.

I look around and notice all the men have eyes on her. So I guess the Carmen Miranda thing is working for her. She's that kind of girl that probably everything works for her. They're my usual weakness. But now is not a good time for weakness, so I shake off the thoughts floating through my mind and make it to the bar, taking a seat, nodding to the bartender, a swell guy with tats, a ripped, black T-shirt and a red bandana hanging out of the back pocket of his completely ridiculous, low-riding, down-below-his-butt pants.

The red and the black. If you're from here, you know that means he's a homie, and mortal enemies with any fool who sports black and blue. I'm not making that up. It's really that dumb. But dumb and dangerous. You gotta respect dangerous.

I make a mental note of what I'm wearing: no red or blue, just a rumpled white T-shirt, leather jacket and black jeans. It's not special, but it's a look that can take me anywhere in LA, up or down the food chain. One of the things I like about So Cal, it's not a dressy place. As long as you're a straight guy and not an agent or actor, you can pretty much get by on not much of a clothing thing.

There's general APPLAUSE and some WOLF-WHISTLING as the homie bartender slides a Corona my way. This is not related to the beer presentation. The lounge singer is taking a bow, working the moment and the crowd, such as it is.

The band strikes up a modern, mariachi-style riff and I watch in the mirror over the bar as the show-stopper gal comes downstage and heads for where I'm sitting. I like her walk. *A lot.* The way she moves, all smooth and silky, and I have to remind myself to stay clear on why I'm in this rat hole.

I start to scan the room, looking for Ramon. I'm actually irritated when Carmen sidles up next to me at the bar and blocks my sight for a good section to my left.

"Hola." She smiles at me and then just as quickly winks at the homie bartender. "Pepe, agua con limon, por favor."

Homie PEPE smiles and sets her up with water with a squeeze of lemon. He slides it her way. She touches his hand in a small gesture of thanks and the boy's smile lights up. I get a flash of what his mom, or his girlfriend sees in him. He actually looks sweet under her touch.

She grabs up a bottle of Tabasco that's sitting on the bar and dabs scary amounts into her drink. She then stirs, slow and enticing, with her trigger finger. To top this *look-at-me* performance off, she then slowly licks the Tabasco and lemon off her finger. Aye, caliente.

She then takes a long, slow drink of her water and makes a production out of it. I try not to watch her, but she's making it impossible not to.

She puts the glass down with an easy motion, then turns to me, leans her elbow on the bar and gets a little close, like in my space. She waits a beat for effect, gives me a curious once-over look and then startles me with:

"You want to sleep with me?"

I do, of course. I'm a guy. And as long as you got all the right parts, and it's abundantly clear Carmen does, the answer's pretty much always the same: You bet. But our timing's off, so it's beside the point of the night.

"I'm good at the moment. Thanks." I look away, feeling some discomfort at whatever her game is and really wanting to concentrate on finding Ramon so I can get on with winning this case.

She moves closer to me and this makes me look back. "At least tell me you like my music."

"Yeah, sure. It's why I come here."

This makes her smile. She laughs, knocking her head back in some exaggerated amusement. And then she turns on another persona, some weird gypsy-psychic-sister routine:

"No. I don't think you like my music. I think you

are here looking for someone. Somebody with a secret. You have that look. A man who finds life full of mysteries, who pretends to have all the answers, but in reality, knows _de nada_."

She gives me a wide-eyed, crazy look and for the first time, I look at her, really, in her eyes and then I get the joke, which is clearly on me: "Kam?"

"Call me Juanita. I'm undercover."

"Are you insane? You can't just do a stakeout alone. It's dangerous to be here. You get that?"

She leans over the bar now, less sexy, more like the girl next door that's closer to her real personality (that is, if she really has _just_ one). "I'm not alone. Milo's with me."

Kam tilts her head right, a couple of times, and I look that way and see Milo, dressed as a Mexican busboy, bussing tables. When he sees me, he nods, like he's James Bond, playing it cool.

"And now I have my new friend, Pepe." Kam wrinkles her nose and smiles at Pepe. When I turn to look at him, he's smiling and nodding, all grimace and tough guy gone. He winks at her and I just want to scream.

"Okay. I'm impressed. That what you want?"

"Of course. You know how much I love approval."

She says that matter-of-factly, no hint of joking. One of things I like about Kam, she does just tell it like it is.

"Okay. Look, hit the bricks. Let me do this. I promise to keep you in the loop," I say, trying to snap some sense into her.

"Oh, I can't go now," she says breezily, "I'm meeting that Ramon guy you mentioned. He supposedly has agreed to meet up with David."

"Ramon Navarro? He's going to talk to you?"

"Yeah. Turns out he's Pepe's third cousin or something…" She smiles at Pepe again.

Pepe leans towards them and all sweet and doing his best sexy, says: "Ramon just gave me the nod. You can go over to him, now."

Pepe indicates toward a booth at the back of the room. Kam and I swing our heads that way and see Ramon, surrounded by his boys and some hookerish women.

Kam smiles at me and turns on her best Carmen Miranda: "Come on, partner, watcha' my back."

And with that, she brazenly heads straight for trouble, blithely unaware of the world she's parading through. I wonder what it's like to go through life like that. And I have half a mind to let her walk this plank solo just to see how this picture turns out. But I don't. Like the sucker I've always been for Kam, I get up and cover her back.

ANOTHER ANGLE – RAMON'S TABLE

As I approach the table where RAMON and his posse are, Michael right behind me, I think I can't believe how much fun I'm having on this stakeout. Undercover is awesome, every bit as much fun as I remember Polly having. And it's not so hard, this finding suspects and stuff. You just have to be smart about tapping your contacts. I had Consuela call a cousin, who called a sister, who called a nephew and within an hour, I had a gig here at *El Diablo* (as the kids call it).

I put this all in motion in less time than it usually takes Carlo to blow my hair out.

I hope Michael sees how well I'm doing here. I do really want him to like our working together again. If this goes well, and I think it will, we are going to have tons of fun at Cade & Barlowe. I look back and see the look on his face. It's a little cross. Perhaps he's not ready for Cade & Barlowe, yet. Like I said, Tauri, they are slow (reluctant) to appreciate change, which is why we Scorpios are so good for them. Our mercurial natures befuddle them, no doubt. And delight (I hope). And it's hard to stay mad when your head is spinning. I know he'll come around. He usually does, at least, he used to.

I stop at the table and give Ramon my best hello-stranger smile, followed quickly with a simple, direct, "Ramon…" trilled just so (I practiced with Consuela to get it just right).

Ramon eyes me appreciatively and then, "Jua-neet-ta." He nods, liking me. And then nods at Michael. "Cop?"

"Private Investigator." Michael says firmly as he steps up to the table next to me.

"I don't talk to you."

"Will you talk to me?" I coo.

Ramon nudges the women out of the booth to make room for me and indicates I should slide in next to him. "If you sit close, perhaps something interesting will slip out."

I slide into the booth, near to him, but not too close. Let's not let weird creep into this, right?

Michael is about to slide in next to me when Ramon waves him off. "You stand, old man."

Michael gives him a grizzled-old-man look. I wonder if Michael is age-sensitive. I'll have to ask him that later.

"I hear this is your turf."

"We don't actually use words like turf." Ramon explains patiently to me, as if he's trying to enlighten me in the ways of his world. "That's like some bad *Starsky and Hutch* Huggybearism."

"I loved Huggy Bear." I really did.

"Me too. Dude was cool." He smiles at me and I guess decides I'm okay based on our mutual love of Huggy Bear. "Yeah, El Diablo, this is my party. What goes down here, goes through me."

"I'm looking for my brother. His name is David Swanson."

Ramon throws me a whassup look. "You're the skinny, pastey-boy's sista?"

"Half. Same pappacita."

Michael is getting impatient, makes the mistake of interjecting: "I hear David's been trying to see you."

Ramon throws a look at Michael. Doesn't answer. The guys get into a stare-off. Mano-a-mano. Great. Measuring stick time. It's on me to redirect this before it gets going in the wrong direction. I reach out and touch Ramon's hand, just so. This has the effect I was hoping for. He turns and smiles my way.

"Do you have any family, Ramon?" I say sadly.

Ramon nods. "Two brothers, four sisters… Eleven nieces. Fifteen nephews. Twenty-seven tias, thirty or so tios and four or five padres. And my madre. She is my rock."

Wow. Didn't see that coming, but it's all a perfect in to where I was going. "So you know how important familia is?"

"La familia is everything."

"Imagine if you only had one brother in your whole world and he was in some kind of danger and only you could help him…"

In order to get this sexy manipulatress just right, I channel Jocelyn and I know I'm spot on. When I glance toward Michael, I can see his jaw hanging open in either disgust or awe at my acting chops. I'm going to go with awe, so I'm not distracted by negativity.

"We're both just kids from the Midwest. Lost in this big city. He's all I have. I know he's into something. I'm trying to help him, before… Well. I don't want him to get hurt. Please. If you know anything."

There's a beat where Ramon steeples his fingers and taps them together, thinking. "He's got something to sell."

"What is it?" Michael growls.

Ramon tosses him a look, then looks back to me. "The stuff that dreams are made of."

I know this reference, am excited to hear it. "The great whatzit."

"Yo… He said he'd come with a sample of the goods. That was two nights ago, but he never showed back. He could be dead by now."

I look to Michael. It's true, David could be dead and then what? Who would win the bet?

"Or…" Ramon's voice gets playful with me, "that could be him walking through the door now."

Ramon nods toward the front entrance. Michael and I swing our looks that way as DAVID SWANSON, 30's, blond, frail-looking and nervous, enters and looks around. He sports a drug addict's calm demeanor, eyes darting at the speed of meth.

When he looks our way, there is recognition and fear. He glances across the room to find another door and instead sees, in a booth at the back, the Mysterious Chinese Man, smoking, watching him.

We turn and see the MCM as well. How did we not earlier? Not like there are a lot of smoking Chinese people in this place.

David appears frozen in fear and then suddenly jerks and jack-rabbits out of there, turning and knocking Milo and his bucket of dishes to the ground. There's a MIGHTY CRASH and then David is gone, out the front and before I can wiggle out of the booth, Michael, like a shot, is out the door, after...

EXT. LA VIVA DIABLO CLUB – BEAT LATER

As I fly out the club's door and into the street, I swivel my head left and right. I hear running FOOTSTEPS ECHOING in the dark and see Michael and Milo running north. Milo stops and turns for me. I start after them and damn it, break a heel, stumble like a klutz and almost fall.

Milo, torn between hot pursuit and helping me, hesitates, takes a step toward me. "No, go. I'm fine. Stay with Michael. Get him!!" I scream with all my might and then realize, wow, this must look freaking bizarre and for sure will make a great story to laugh with Lumm over `tini's.

Milo nods and runs at top speed, gaining on Michael just as David turns the far corner.

It occurs to me, if I'm fast, and I am, I run a fair bit, I can round the near corner to me and surprise David, if on the off-chance he makes a bad move and rounds the block back my way. You never know, given his panic, he might run in circles.

I rip my dress to give me room to move (sorry,

Stan-Darling), take off my shoes and head south, running barefoot in my crazy Carmen outfit, throwing myself entirely into the moment. I feel like I'm flying. Abandon is an amazing high.

I pay no attention to the black caddy that is slowly coming up behind me, don't at first notice the big goon that is standing in the back seat, hulking over the convertible's open edge…

EXT. DOWNTOWN LA – EMPTY STREET

I am just barely able to keep up with that loser, David. I could almost catch him if I could just dig out a little more speed in my old legs. If only I hadn't given up staying in shape for the privilege of being lazy and putting on a few.

I look back and see Milo gaining on me. But no Kam. That shoots a little worry in me. I know she's a runner. She should be passing me by now. Why isn't she? I know she came out of the club, just behind me. I heard her screaming at the kid.

At the end of the short block, David turns south, essentially making a U.

The block we are on now is darker and crappier than the club's block—either that, or it all seems darker because not enough oxygen is getting to my brain. Geez. I'm sucking air bad. I just really want this chase to end.

For a moment, I actually hope somebody will call "cut..." I hate myself for even thinking that.

Milo passes me. "You okay?"

I nod, wave him on and try to pull out one more burst of whatever I got left in the tank, which is nothing, not even fumes.

David passes an unbolted, abandoned newspaper dispenser and tosses it at Milo and me as he runs past it. We both scatter to move around the rolling obstacle.

David heads into an alley and down the dark. Milo and I approach carefully. Bad things happen in alleys and I'm not all that interested in dying in one.

As I poke my head around the edge, scanning the alley from a safe vantage, GUNSHOTS ring out. But, weirdly, not from David, not here in the alley. They sound at least a block away, maybe. And, given the neighborhood, not that much of a surprise.

My rule of thumb generally is, if the bullets aren't flying at me, I'm not that concerned about them.

By the barest of light at the end, I can see David scale a chain link fence and hop over it. I stop. I'm done.

Milo, I realize, is standing next to me, pressed up against the wall, eyes on the street behind us. At least the kid's got my back. "Do you want me to go after him?"

"Whatever, Kid. I'm not going down there. I'm not getting killed trying to catch this guy." I'm still sucking air.

"Darn…" I hear Milo say and realize, he's not even breathing that hard. I hate young people.

"You heard those gunshots, right?"

I nod.

"What do you think?" He appears overly concerned with something that has nothing to do with us.

"Downtown LA." I say, as if that explains random gunfire.

Gunfire is easy to ignore, but a woman screaming bloody-murder, less so.

Milo and I both hear the SCREAMS, a women's voice, not that far away.

We move out of the alley and take a few steps into the street just in time to see a black Cadillac convertible sail through the lit intersection not twenty-feet from us. There's no mistaking that some ginormous guy, inside the car, is holding Kam, outside the car, about two feet above the ground.

Her legs are flailing and she is screaming. Her screams are then muffled when the goon tosses her into the backseat of the car. The caddy zooms off into the night.

Milo and I are stunned and stop in our tracks. Then suddenly, not sure what hits me, but I bolt after the car, moving faster than I would have thought possible. By the time I turn the corner, the caddy is nowheresville. So gone.

Milo runs up next to me.

"Was that...? Milo can't even say her name.

I simply nod.

"Oh wow. That can't be good."

I simply look at Milo. I mean, what do you say at a time like this?

FADE OUT.

END ACT THREE

ACT FOUR

FADE IN:

INT. STORAGE ROOM – MORNING

My eyes flutter open and I see light, fortunately not the bright, white one that calls you home. This is the soft, hazy light of the dawn of another warm, LA day. I have a moment where I don't really know where I am or how I got here. I'm pretty sure I'm not at my favorite hotel. This room has acoustic ceiling tiles, is stocked with what appears to be Chinese food take-out cartons and the smell coming from somewhere might just be dead-something soup. I bite my lip and think, which isn't that easy as my brain seems heavily fogged…

It takes me a second to orient and I realize I am lying on a futon mattress, not covered by sheets (eeew) in what appears to be some kind of restaurant storage room.

I sit up, too quickly, and feel simultaneously woozy and nauseous. I steady myself by placing both hands behind me on the futon. It's only then that I tune into the fact that my head is pounding and I have dry mouth like I've just crawled through the Sahara.

I'm startled like a heroin junkie (what??) when I place my hand on my head and there is something like a basket of fruit festooned on me. I stagger up, which ain't easy, and toddle over to a mirror on the wall.

As I approach, I get a good look at myself—eye-carumba! What a hot mess. I know I should be horrified. I got plastic fruit on my head, askew, mind you, held in place by a platoon of brave and steady bobby-pin soldiers, fighting the good fight to hold the line (and doing an astoundedly good job with so few men). My makeup is rubbed and blended across one cheek, not in a good way and raccoon eyes, nothing! I'm sporting nearly a full Boy Wonder mask. I think I might cry and am taken by surprise when I simply start to laugh, hysterically.

I'm still high from whatever they shot into me.

Oh yeah, and then the memories tumble from I don't know where exactly: A shot, a humongous needle… A humongous guy. Shrek. The Caddy. Singing at the club. Ramon. Oh, Michael. He's going to be mad at me… I hate it when Michael's mad at me and he's been mad at me for what, like ten years. This getting kidnapped while working on his case is not going to help.

There's a window and I'm just tall enough to get one eye over the ledge and look out. Chinatown—Where they say, you may think you know what you're dealing with, but believe me, you don't. That's from the movie, I realize, and I might be wise to keep that in mind. Not a big surprise, considering the contents of the room I'm in. But why Chinatown? What's here? Why me? And what in god's name is that awful smell?

The door opens and I turn to find a young Chinese man, dressed in a really beautifully cut and tailored classic suit. Must've been one hell of a tailor, because the man is Sumo size and getting a suit to fit this nicely on such a Jabba-the-Hutt takes some really fine, old-school talent.

The man is cherubic, friendly looking. He stares at me intensely, which I usually don't mind, but something about the way he is doing it is creepy. Shrek, I can see, is hovering behind. And then it hits me and I blurt out without any ability to filter: "Fatman!"

I wag my finger at him as I move a step closer. I am unsteady, like a college coed on a Friday night. "You are fat. So fat. I'm sorry. I'm just maybe a little bit still high from whatever, you know."

FATMAN nods, and indicates for Shrek to help me to a chair. "Have her sit."

Shrek makes his way to me and expects to guide me over. Instead, I wrap my arms around him and hug him like a long-lost friend. "Shrek! Mmm. You are so warm. And you smell nice. Like soap. I love that." I hug him tightly. He actually hugs me back.

"What are you doing?" Fatman barks at him.

"Sorry," Shrek mumbles and then he tries to lead me to the chair, but I don't wanna move. So instead, he brings the chair to me and jams it under me, at my knees, and I begin to sink into a sit position and when my butt hits the chair, I let out an audible sigh.

"How much did you give her?"

"The usual…"

"Do you not see her size?"

"I just did what I always do."

"We are lucky she is still alive." Fatman sighs unhappily. He doesn't seem that content with his help.

"I'm glad I'm still alive. Yeah. Thanks." I say to no one in particular, while blowing a stray wisp of my hair out of my eyes. It floats back again so I blow up again, trying to get it away. I do this maybe two or three times until:

"Enough!" demands the fat man, startling me.

When I look at him, he looks to Shrek, exasperated.

"I told you. She's a handful." Shrek shrugs to his boss.

"Ms. Cade…?"

"Yes, Mr. Fatman? Is that what I call you? I mean, it seems, well, unkind. And I don't want you to think me unkind. I'm not unkind. Ask anybody. I'm kind. I mean, sometimes I can be oblivious and maybe a tad bit, just a little bit, well, self-centered. I try not to be, but…"

"Yes. Fatman will be fine. Can you focus, please?"

"I really can't. I am totally whoo, three sheets to the wind, whatever that expression actually means. I don't know. Do you? Well, point is, I don't put synthetic compounds in me, ever. I obviously don't handle them all that well. I'm extremely anti-drug. And frankly, I find it outrageous you would have your thug, sorry big guy, your thug inject me without first asking if it were alright."

I'm up and in his face, indignant at what has transpired. And wobbly. I return to the chair and sit.

Fatman shoots a look to Shrek, displeased with, well, everything.

"Oh, I'm sorry. Is there some kind of code of conduct for kidnap victims? Did I miss the memo specifying what, cooperative, maybe chipper and pleasant in captivity?

"I would settle for silent." Fatman glares at me.

"Yeah, well, I am not exactly the silent type."

Fatman crosses his little arms on his chest and sighs. He regroups and smiles pleasantly my way. "Ms. Cade. You have not been kidnapped. You have merely been invited here for a chat. I wanted to meet you."

"Really? Are you a fan of my show?" I can't help but get excited when I think one is near.

"Not at all. I disliked your show very much. But I do like that you and Mr. Barlowe are working together again."

"Why? What's it to you?"

"David Swanson is your client, correct?"

"I really can't confirm or deny that. There's a private investigator's code or something. I'm not really sure. I haven't exactly had time to study the handbook. I wonder if there is a handbook."

"I have no patience for your rambling. I want the three-legged cat. I will pay you twenty-thousand dollars for it."

I WHISTLE. "That's some dough. Gotta be worth a lot more than that. Is that really your best offer?"

He smiles, not the nice kind. "I will go as high as…"

"Wait, wait… Is that my cell?" I hear a distant RINGING and I follow it and find my phone stuffed under the futon.

I grab it out and answer. "Lumm! No, I'm not home. I had a wild night. No, not that kind. Actually, I think I've been kidnapped."

Fatman tosses me a look. "You have not."

I look to Fatman and over the phone whisper to him: "Are you going to kill me or harm me in any way?"

"Not today."

"I think I'm okay." I say back into the phone. "By some guy they call the Fatman… Oh, yeah, Big. Huge. Totally unhealthy… Un huh. Yeah. I'll tell him." I look over at the Fatman and he's clearly doing a slow-burn to a state of intense anger. "Okay, thanks for trying. Let me know."

I hang up, bummed. "I'm having trouble getting this audition for a part I really want. It's in my ex-husband's movie… He actually wrote the part for me. Sure, it was a long time ago, but I gotta think, I could still play it. Right?" I look at the guys for some support. "It's not even that big of a part." Hmm, still nothing. Neither Shrek nor Fatman respond.

"Okay. Well, my friend, she says to let you know, she can get you some really great Ayurvedic herbs that could help you slim down safe and fast."

Still no response. This is a cold room.

"Got it. Now is not the time. Okay, back to the cat thing. Whassup with that? You were talking price. Talk high. I might listen." I smile, like, sure, I got this. It's all going my way now.

"Fifty-thousand dollars."

"For a cat?"

"A very special cat. Do we have a deal?"

"Sure."

The Fatman nods and turns to exit and before he can squeeze his rotundness through the door, I ask this one little thing: "Could you just give me a tiny hint where the three-legged meower might be?"

He turns and looks at me with a firm and fixed stare. "That is your problem now. You have forty-eight hours. Either you bring me the cat or, *The New Adventures of Polly & Jake* will be cancelled."

Oh. He says that so villainously. I bite my lip. I take that to mean permanent cancellation, like cement-shoes permanent.

Uh oh. Now Michael is going to be super-pissed at me for drawing a death-threat. I wonder if I can possibly find some reasonable way to maybe not mention to Michael that unless we find some three-legged cat, one of us might be dead in two-days' time.

I get anxious just thinking about having to have that talk with him.

And then, the smell of whatever that horrible thing cooking is, gets me, and I ralph, you know, puke, like volcano-style, all over that Fatman's nice suit. He looks at me, I think stunned by this turn of events.

And I know I should feel bad about it. I mean, it's an awful thing to do to somebody. But, considering what he put me through last night and the small fact that he's just threatened to kill me, well, maybe I feel like he kind of deserves it, little bit.

"Get away from me!" He thunders, apparently coming out of the shock. He stumbles out of the storage room and well, I don't know where he goes after that. Shrek blocks the doorway so I can't exit and gives me a look and I think, maybe, a small smile.

INT. MICHAEL'S OFFICE - MORNING

Officer Gina D'Amico leans against the doorway, in her civvies: jeans, tight, sexy T-shirt, hair down, badge clipped to her belt.

I gotta say, it's a winning look. I was right, out of that dog of a uniform, every bit the show-stopper that Kam is.

LA women, nothing to complain about in the looks department (plenty in other areas).

"The vic at the park, Peter Lorring. Swanson's cell-mate." She talks to me like we're old friends and she's just passing the time with chit chat.

I like that familiarity with her. I don't know where it comes from and, for some reason, it doesn't bother me.

"I'm just guessing, but his untimely demise is not a random act of violence," she says with just a hint of lightness about the matter.

I am at my desk, looking out the window and at the same time, glancing over to her, in the doorway, from time to time, nodding, indicating I'm listening. I half am. My other half of brain power is consumed with worry about Kam. It's been over twelve hours since she was taken. No calls for ransom, no calls at all. That usually adds up to something pretty rough. I try to keep my mind off the possibilities, with this conversation with Gina.

"What was Lorring in for?"

"FBI pinched him smuggling tiger parts."

She comes into the room a step or two and looks around, trying to get a sense of me, where I work, what it says about me. It's not just a cop move, but a gal who might be interested move. But it's hard to tell if it's just her habit or something more.

I'm not particularly good at understanding interested signs from women. Much like the ponies, I usually don't pick up on the important indicators until the bets are lost and the tickets torn.

"He'd be a middle man in that. Why would the Feds go after him?"

"Looking for a bigger fish?" She gives a shrug.

I rub my face, realize I need a shave. I didn't go home last night, just came straight to the office with the kid, Milo. Not much we could do other than call the cops. At this point, we don't even know who took Kam, or why. So, I focus on other things.

"Bigger prize." I say turning and giving her a wan smile. I want to at least indicate gratitude. She didn't have to come here on her time off. That is pretty aces of her. "What if Lorring was smuggling more than tiger parts and went to jail before he could deliver?"

"That'd make sense…" She nods. "He shares a little

after-dark, jailhouse sweet talk with Swanson..."

"...Swanson gets out first, high-tails it to the great whatzit."

Gina smiles, curious, at me: "What's a whatzit?"

"Something Kam said at the club."

"Somebody thinks she knows something. That must be why they nabbed her."

Something about the way Gina says that actually seems comforting.

"And you got nothing on the car?"

"You gave me nothing to go on. Black convertible caddy?"

I shrug. She's right. Could be a million cars like that and maybe the one they used was stolen. It's a lousy lead.

"What about her cell?"

"Unlisted. Not in her name. Standard for the famous. I can't locate her records, can't ask for a records tap."

I look through my office door to the desk beyond. Effie is there, pretending not to listen to every word Gina and I exchange. "Effie, try her house again."

Effie comes over to the doorway and gives me a shrug. "I've left four messages."

"Maybe number five will annoy her husband enough to wake his lazy—"

"No husband." Effie interrupts me.

"What?"

"Splitsville. I ran her through Google, IMDb. All the sad, personal details of her marriage are there. *People* and *US* ran pretty decent full page articles complete with super pathetic photos of Kam at her worst. At least I hope they're her worst. I mean, some of those pics were pretty awful. You gotta feel for her. Her rat husband was having an affair with the lead actress on the show he worked on after yours. You didn't know any of this?"

"She didn't say anything to me."

"Did you ask?" Effie gives me a look. She knows I didn't.

There's a beat of uncomfortable. I feel like a heel, but I don't know why. Why would I ask her how her life is, I don't really care. At least I didn't, until about twelve hours ago.

"What about the house… helper?" Gina asks Effie.

"I'm sure she knows."

"Not about the divorce, Ef… Can we reach her?"

Effie shakes her head. "Didn't you get a number from her at the park?"

"She gave me Ms. Cade's home number."

"Effie, get the phone book out and…"

"No way. Do you know how many Gonzalezes there must be? If you want to call everyone in the LA phonebook, be my guest. But futile-waste-of-time is not in my job description." Effie gives me a look and then goes back to her desk and does whatever she does out there.

I turn to see Gina giving me another bemused look. "You got woman troubles, my friend."

Now she's teasing me. I'm too tired to object. And I need coffee. Something that doesn't get made in my office crappot.

"I gotta go. I caught the a-m shift." She says with what seems like a hint of reluctance.

I nod at her and as she turns to go, she turns back. "I almost forgot..." She grabs a clear, plastic bag out of her purse. It has my gun. She hands it back to me. "All clear."

She has me sign a release stating I received the return of my weapon.

"Thanks." I say surprised at the special and amazingly quick service.

"If there's anything I can do. I hope you'll call me." She hands me her PD card. I like the way her hand breezes mine as I take it.

And with a smile, she heads out, passing Effie and is gone.

Effie is in my office like a shot. "She was so flirting..."

I give Effie a get-out-of-here look. "She's a cop."

"A pretty cop. A smoking hot cop..."

"You want her number?"

"If I went that way, I would. Why aren't you interested?"

"If you haven't noticed, we have a crisis on our hands."

"I thought you didn't even like the actress. What's with all the worry?"

And I have to think, why do I feel so bad about this? And I realize: "If I hadn't said yes to that dumb interview, none of this would be happening. If she gets hurt, it's on me."

Effie nods and heads out, then turns back at the door and fixes a look on me. "Why did you?"

"Clients. We need them." Simple enough.

The front door (which is currently sporting a plywood plug where the glass should be) opens and Jocelyn comes in.

"Speaking of which…" Effie gives a nod towards the front.

"Just sit at your desk and pretend to not be listening."

Effie nods and returns to her desk, passing Jocelyn in the process. "Ms. Swanson…"

"Good morning, Effie." Jocelyn says sweetly. She then turns to me and fixes a broad, enticing smile on me as she enters my office and takes a seat in the guest chair across from my desk. In a flash, I realize everything Kam said about her is right. There is something very off about Ms. Swanson and, even unidentified, it still kind of gives me the creeps.

"I just got your message. Any news?" She pretends to care, but the vibe is not really.

"Where have you been?" I sit on the edge of my desk so that I'm in her space, a little above her. This is a power position and I'm here for a reason.

"With a friend."

"I thought you were new in town."

She gives me a look. Doesn't like to be questioned. "I am. But I know people."

I simply look at her. For a long, intense moment and it unnerves her, or at least, I am hoping it does.

"Have I done something to make you distrust me? If so, tell me what, so I can convince you you're wrong."

This is a game to her and one she thinks she's

winning. I get up and move to the window, look out at the sand, the water, the day as it breaks over Santa Monica. It's too pretty a place for the sludge she's peddling.

"This case. What you've told me... The pieces don't fit." And I turn and look at her, really for the first time. And I don't like what I see. "You have been lying to me since you first walked in that door."

"Of course I haven't..."

"You're lying now." I say this maybe a tad too forcefully. She pauses, pursing her lips, debating if she should let the next lie gently cross them.

I just want to get her to tell the truth. So, I grab her by both shoulders and shake her roughly.

"Admit it, damn it. You're lying. Tell me the truth or..."

I notice Effie looking at me through the open door, and I think she might be shocked, disapproving as I rough up the client. Instead, she gives me the thumbs up and mouths "yeah..." as I shake Jocelyn one good, last time, hard.

"Okay. Okay..." Jocelyn shakes me off of her and moves away. "I am lying."

At a safe distance from me, she regroups. You can see it in her eyes. A double down on whatever tale she's gonna spin next.

"I do know what David is doing. People are after him."

She begins to weep, but I'm not buying it. Or I don't care, or both.

"Stop with the tears, sister. I'm not interested and I

don't believe they're anything, but crocodile."

She bucks up, turning off the pity faucet like a flip of switch.

"These people want what Peter Lorring was smuggling?" I tip I know something because at some point, someone in this room has to.

She looks impressed: "The very thing."

"The stuff that dreams are made of."

"That's how it was described to me."

"So, all this is about *that*, whatever *that* turns out to be. I don't like working in the dark."

Jocelyn stands and smooths out her outfit. "I've told you all I know."

"Doubtful."

"Okay. How about I've told you all I think you need to know."

"That I'll buy."

We do a full on Mexican stand-off, gunning for each other with our eyes.

"Now what?"

I can't stand to look at her mug another second, "Get out. But stay where I can find you."

"You're still working for me?"

"I'm working for myself. To find Kam and if, in the process, I find your loser brother, then yeah, I'll take your money."

"You're a nasty piece of work, aren't you?"

"Is that what you expected when you came to me?"

"It's what I counted on."

She places a check on my desk. "I'll double that if,

when you find David, you let me know before the police. If you don't, or if you double cross me in anyway, that check won't make. So don't go spending it before this is settled."

I pick up the check. It's for ten large, way over our agreed price. I nod. She leaves and I think, I should've shaken that money tree earlier.

I move to my office window and watch as Jocelyn exits my building and gets into a car that was waiting for her. Who is driving it? What other sucker does she have on the line? The car drives off and I find myself feeling sorry for whomever the poor sap is. And I wonder, who is she really, and what in the hell are we all chasing?

I need coffee and a shot of something to help me think and I know just the place to find my tonic.

EXT. OCEAN FRONT WALK – MORNING

My office, I think I mentioned before, is on the north end stretch of the Venice ocean front walk. Most tourists who come this far north get bored by the normalcy.

All the entertaining weirdos stay south of here, nearer to the Washington Boulevard area where they can successfully busk for cash all day long, almost any day of the year.

The tourists that make it this far, either keep walking, hoping the Santa Monica pier is a lot closer than it's gonna be or they turn round and go back to the main area.

No one lingers. This is just a place to move through.

The places around my office are rundown and sketchy. They are primarily occupied by the underground rentals set: hippies, surfers and derelicts who spend their days smoking pot, walking their mangy mutts, strumming guitars on balconies and gardening in their tiny front porch areas.

Some of the bottom units are being used for businesses. T-shirts seem to be a big winner out here and head shops. Hookahs, apparently, are all the rage again, because hey, nothing says young and stupid like sucking flavored smoke into perfectly good lungs from shared inhaler hoses. This way we can all get cancer and herpes together. Kumbaya, my friends.

Oh, I know I sound like a guy who doesn't know how to have a good time. And it's true, the bitter in me seems to be around more than not these days. But I know how to have a good time, have had too many good times, which is where all the wisdom comes from post-30.

And I'm no saint or some LA metrosexual who treats his body like a temple. I treat my body like a 7-Eleven. I pretty much just stuff it with junk and see how the day goes. Which is why I'm here, now, at my favorite morning stop: Ocean Walk Cafe. When I need to clear my head, this is usually my local place of choice.

EXT. OCEAN WALK CAFÉ - CONTINUOUS

The Ocean Walk is an open air café just off the path. It's really just several cheap chairs and little round tables that wobble in front of a ratty apartment that during the day breaks every zoning code known to Venice. But the city thankfully leaves it alone and the view can't be beat. The service is actually not bad either.

As I grab a seat, JEROME, the owner's kid, comes over to me: "Regular or special, Mr. Barlowe?"

Jerome has a light Irish accent that always throws me a bit. He's a sort of black kid. His dad is white and his mom black, from some island that was once owned by the UK. I can never remember which one and really, it doesn't matter since she's not my mom.

Jerome's nineteen, got what I think might be a Euro-style vibe to him, big hair and dresses hipster: hats, jackets and tight pants. He reminds me of *Style Council*, a band I used to like in college. He's a good kid, a hard worker and I don't know why I think this, but I believe he'll go far. Wherever far is for him. I don't think he knows. Right now, he's going to SMCC (Santa Monica City College) and doing pick up production work in some post house when he's not working here.

Before I can answer him, his dad, ROGER, appears at my table with two coffee mugs and he puts one in front of me. Roger is a robust Irish man of maybe 40, but due to his habit of drinking daily and copiously, looks closer to 50. He's ruddy-faced a good portion of the time and brusque. He doesn't really like people and he doesn't tolerate much. We get along great: soul mates of the Venice beach board-walk.

"Can't you tell, Jerome? Today this man needs a special."

"That obvious?" I ask.

"Written all over you. What's your trouble today, Michael?" And with his heavy brogue, Roger sounds like what we all think an Irish priest talks like. "Why are you here at my establishment drinking fine whiskey at nine in the morning?"

He taps his coffee mug to mine.

"How fine is it?"

"Taste it and see."

I do and it's good. Just what the doctor ordered. It's smooth and warm and more whiskey than coffee—and I'm not complaining. I can feel it relax me the moment it hits my tongue.

Roger always has a little something for the coffee. A regular would have meant Jameson. A good brand. But the special, well, that is whatever bottle Roger is trying at the moment and he prides himself on trying some pretty exceptional brown liquors. Today apparently it's something called Tyrconnell. And it's spectacular. Lucky for me, Roger is a man who believes the finer things in life should be shared with friends.

"Damn fine cup of coffee." I say and nod.

"This a case, Michael, or woman that's got you down?"

"Both."

"Aye, you'll be needing a double-special today." He turns to wave Jerome for more. I wave Roger off.

"No. Can't. I just needed to get out of the office a bit and inhale a pick me up."

I look out over the ocean. Let the light, salty breeze hit my face and I feel calm for a moment. Then I look back to Roger. "I wish I could, but too much is going on to dedicate my day to the Tyrconnell haze. "

"That is a shame. The Tyrconnell haze is lovely way to pass the day."

We share smiles. He shrugs and sips the rest of his

morning special.

We sit a beat in silence and just enjoy the place, the view, the moment. There are not many people I can sit with in silence and feel totally comfortable and at ease. It's nice and I appreciate it for what it is.

"Can I do anything to help?"

"You already have." I smile and I throw a five on the table as I get up to head back to reality.

Roger picks it up and waves it back at me. "Must we do this every time? You know your money is no good here."

I did a small case for Roger back in the day, for free, really a nothing track down of his ex-wife, which just happened to prove she had remarried down in Mexico and that voided her right for spousal alimony. From that day forward, Roger won't take a dime from me. But, Jerome will. And that's the joke of it. Jerome, in college, needs every dime his dad spends on expensive whiskey. So, why we toss the fiver back and forth, Jerome quietly steps up and pockets it.

"Thanks." And he heads back into the apartment, five dollars richer. See, smart kid.

As I'm about to head back to my office, Roger puts a hand on my arm, worried.

"There were some men here earlier, asking about you."

"What'd they ask, exactly?"

"Just off hand, like they wanted me to think they weren't really looking for you, but they're not that smooth. Amateurs of some sort. Just not sure the sort."

"What'd they look like?"

"Kids. Nothing special. One fancies himself a tough

guy. You can tell from his demeanor and the fact that he refused to speak directly to me. This mean something to you?"

"Well, maybe." And it does and I know who they are. They're not connected to this case and I just hope I don't run into them today. I'm not in the mood and I don't have what they want (money). I thank Roger with a tap on his shoulder and head back, hoping that when I get there, Effie has some news about Kam.

EXT. OCEAN FRONT WALK – MOMENT LATER

I am mildly buzzed from the morning special, which means I'm feeling good and not paying that much attention to what's around me. Big mistake.

As I approach my office, just a building away, I am grabbed from behind and pulled into the alley and pushed against the wall, hard, by the kids Roger has warned me of.

"Yo, Benny. Easy."

I know the kids, of course. They handle collections for a poker game I'm a regular at.

BENNY is large and the one who fancies himself a tough guy. Actually, he is a tough guy, like Philly tough, and dumb as the Liberty Bell. It's amazing he's found the perfect job for his skills.

The other guy is a puzzle to me. He seems cultured, smart and capable and what he's doing being a bookie's muscle is a mystery. But I have heard, through others, he likes violence. So I'm guessing that's his hook here.

Benny holds me to the wall, tight, with one massive hand on my throat, as SIMON looks at me and considers his options here.

"You know what we want."

"I don't have it."

"You borrowed two from my boss. Not his fault you got beat by the river."

"Yeah. Still. I don't have it."

"When will you have it?"

"Simon, be a man. If you are here to teach me a lesson, just freaking hit me and get it over with." I know it's coming and I just don't have the patience for Simon to go through whatever script he's got in his head.

"Benny will do the hitting."

Benny stands back and is gonna pow me one when Simon puts a hand on his arm. "Dude, not in his face. He's a pretty boy. Let's not ruin the one thing he has going for him."

"Thanks," I say and mean it. I'm not that vain, but all the same, would be bummed to break a nose or worse. And the face hurts, like a mo-fo when hit. Unfortunately, I have had some experience with this.

Benny hits me gut-high, full and hard and I double over in real pain, find it hard to breath. I guess he knocked the wind out of me. And I think I wish I knew how to do that to a guy. It would really come in handy in my business. As I come up from my doubled over, Simon sees something in my jacket pocket and flicks it out.

"What the hell, Mikey... You're holding out on us?"

He's got the check that Jocelyn gave me.

"It's not good, man. You don't want it."

"If there's a fool here, in this alley, it's not me." And with that, Simon hits me in the face, full, at my right eye.

"I'm keeping this as a down payment on future muck ups. You still owe us the two grand."

He and Benny head out the other end of the alley. I watch as their shapes turn to silhouettes and then disappear as they turn onto Speedway, the street that runs just behind the houses on the ocean side. I sigh because I know when the check bounces, I'll get another beating. I'm not sure the thrill of winning at poker is worth this. But after giving up the ponies, poker is the only real bona fide vice I have left. I'm reluctant to throw it out and live life without the highs and the lows. See, we all got something.

EXT. MICHAEL'S OFFICE – CONTINUOUS

I hold my eye and squint, as if that might mitigate the pain (it doesn't). It feels like it's swelling already. Gonna be a shiner.

I am moving, maybe not all that steadily, towards my office. And as I get to just in front of the entrance door, I hear a car moving unmistakably fast. Too fast for the area. I look up and see the black caddy has just turned off Pacific and is careening towards me.

Now, where I'm standing is the end of the road There's path and sand and those are not great for cars. At the rate they're rolling, they aren't going to be able to make a stop. I look around and see maybe two or three people (including myself) that might die instantly if that car flies through here. And what do I do? I just stand in place and watch. I guess the whiskey has impaired my flight instincts.

I'm relieved when the black caddy makes a fast jerk left and slides and skitters to a tread-marked stop just long enough to push Kam out of the back seat of the car. I watch as she rolls and hits the curb, not all that gently.

Strangely, the big goon who rolled Kam out winces when she hits the curb, like he feels badly about it. He looks up and sees me watching and gives a little wave just as the car speeds away, down Speedway, ironically (maybe. I don't know. Like Alanis Morrisette, I'm not real clear on how to use that word).

I run over to Kam. She is blindfolded and damn if she doesn't still have that fruit basket on her head. Amazing.

EXT. MICHAEL'S OFFICE – ON KAM

"Oh wow. That is so not cool! You guys suck!" I yell out to no one in particular as I try to roll myself up. But ow, I'm hurting all over. I find it hard to actually right myself. My body is definitely not used to being abused like this.

Suddenly, somebody's hands are on me and I start to panic and fight them off and then a voice floats through my defenses.

"Kam… Kam, it's me…"

And I know that's Michael, which means I'm okay. I'm safe.

He must have taken off my blindfold because suddenly everything is so damn bright. I have to squint and it takes a second for my eyes to adjust and then I see him clearly. Wow. He looks bad.

"Are you okay?"

We both say to each other at the same time.

"What happened to you?"

We both say to each other at the same time."

"I'm okay." I get out first and then he nods, same for him.

And then he does something totally wonderful and unexpected. He hugs me tight.

"Okay. This is nice." And I hug him back tightly.

"You smell like you've been drinking?" I say as I burrow into his chest, tucked safely into his arms.

"You smell like vomit." He says, not mean, just like it is.

"Oh that…"

"Did they hurt you?"

"They made me sleep on a futon without sheets."

This makes him laugh. "Kam…"

I pull out and look at him. It's nice to see him smile, even if liquor's needed to ply it out of him.

"Other than that, it wasn't so bad." We're having a nice thing here, no reason to rush into the 'hey, they're going to kill us' part of the story.

He then (finally) does me a huge favor and undoes a bobby pin or two and removes that turban thing from my head. My hair falls down loose and feels free.

"That's better," he says.

"Much." I agree. You have no idea what it's like to have something like that on your head through such stress.

We share a look. We are having a weird moment of, I don't know what, connection, out here in a dirty curb in Venice. Not exactly the way I dreamed Michael and I might share some electricity again, but considering the last twelve hours, I'm damn happy to be hanging out here in the gutter with him.

I look down at my feet and see a pair of bright white and red striped paper slippers, the kind you might buy at the salon if you forgot to wear your own slip-ons.

Having lost my shoes last night in the chase of David, it was somewhat thoughtful of my abductors to provide me a new pair for the ride home. And, I am happy my feet are somewhat covered because they are filthy and I don't want Michael to see my dirty feet.

I lean my head against Michael a little bit more, close my eyes enjoying this. He stiffens, sitting up a little straighter and he releases his embrace of me just a bit. Uh oh, I think. He's just realizing he's actually hugging me and is going to pull out. I try to wrap my arms around him in a way to make it hard for him to end this (I'm liking it).

"Hey!" He yells, really loudly in my ear.

"Okay. Sorry…" I say as I hug a little less.

I am surprised when he bolts up and sort of pushes me off of him and starts to run from me.

"Hey!" He yells again and he takes off down the street.

At a loss, I sort of shrug and say to myself: "Was it something I said?"

"No. It was the Mysterious Chinese Man."

I turn to see Effie standing in the office doorway.

"He was watching you guys from the alley."

I stand up and sigh. "Oh. This is where we chase again." I remove my lovely paper slippers, knowing I can't run in them. "You coming?"

Effie shakes her head, no way: "I'm just the office girl. You can probably catch them by going up Speedway."

She points to the street where Shrek dropped me.

I nod and take off up the block, barefoot and sprinting again and all I can think about is when this day is over if I can book a blissful, peppermint soothing foot wrap at the hot springs because man, my feet are killing me.

EXT. VENICE STREETS – VARIOUS

As I turn onto Speedway, I can see Michael ahead running and gaining on the MCM, who fortunately does not seem all that fast a runner. He is, however, cagey and does a pretty good dodge and weave. He takes a left into an alley and I know that he'll come out one block up. I dodge left at the street corner and burn my last stores of muscle fat to beat him to the next block.

As I turn right onto the next block, I am surprised to find that Michael has already caught him and is in the process of throwing him to the ground, fist at the ready, threatening a serious beat-down on the man.

I run up just as the MCM falls to his knees and cowers in fear of Michael striking him. He has one arm raised above his head and he pleads with Michael in a low, firm babble of some foreign language.

"Who are you? Why the hell are you following us?" Michael screams at the man.

The MCM, upon a closer look, is elderly, maybe mid-40s, portly and without his Luger, clearly afraid of us. He continues to insistently babble in that language, which I suddenly realize, I can understand.

I step forward and babble at him in Mandarin Chinese. My Mandarin is rusty so I think I am saying something like: "It's okay. We won't hurt you." And, possibly: "Please hold the MSG. I am food-sensitive."

Both Michael and the man look to me.

"What language is that?" Michael asks.

"Mandarin." The man answers.

"You know Mandarin?" Michael always seems amazed I'm not a complete idiot.

Panting, I nod. "Remember, episode two-dash-thirty-two: *The Case of the Half Moon Murder*. I was a geisha."

"Ah, geisha are Japanese women." The MCM says with a proper English accent.

"I know! And I objected to that during the shoot. But our writers said nobody would notice."

The MCM babbles angrily in Mandarin, fast and rapid.

"What's he saying now?"

"I'm not sure but I think, it'd be all bleeped out."

"Ask him why he's following us." Michael nods toward the man.

The man stops babbling and looks at Michael. "Did you not just notice I speak perfectly good English?"

"He does." I say, backing him, even though it's sort of a pointless comment.

"Okay. Why are you following us? What do you want from us?"

"The Golden Dragon."

"Now…" I say, getting excited, "that's new."

"We don't have any golden dragon."

"It belongs to my family. It is my duty to get it back. I will do anything to get it."

"Including kill us?" I say, breathlessly.

"Kam..? Let's not give him any ideas."

"I'm just asking…"

"Well," says the MCM, "I would prefer not to, but if that were my only option…"

"It's not. We don't have it. We don't know anything about it." Michael makes clear.

"This have something to do with a three-legged cat?" I blurt out, to Michael's surprise.

"Yes. It holds the key!"

Michael swivels his head between me and the MCM. "What cat?"

"The three-legged cat." Both the MCM and I say to Michael at the same time.

"How do you know about this cat?"

"The fat man wants it."

"Who?"

"Fatman bad man. Not to be trusted. He will kill you for it."

"Yeah, he mentioned that, sort of." I say with a look to Michael, because I know he's looking at me. "I'll fill you in on that later."

"Yeah. That might be good." Poor Michael, he's totally not up to speed here. He just looks at me and the MCM.

"Fatman offered me fifty thousand dollars for it."

Michael WHISTLES.

"I know." I say, with enthusiasm.

"I will pay twice what he's—

And before he can finish that sweet offer, a late model sedan rounds the corner and guns it for us. We three exchange '*uh oh*' looks and then scramble for it.

The car careens off a chain-link fence, sparks flying and draws close. Michael has one shot to either drag down the MCM and hold onto him, or... to protect me from the oncoming hunk of Detroit exceptionalism.

Michael grabs my hand and throws his body against me and rolls us out of the path of the oncoming metal missile. We roll up to a property line wall and huddle close as the vehicle thankfully flies past us and SCREECHES as it turns the corner and disappears.

Big sighs. When the dust settles and all is quiet, we look at each other.

Michael is lying on top of me, at the edge of the alley's pavement. The MCM is gone. I can see that Michael is visibly disappointed that I'm the only person he's left here with.

Without a word, Michael stands up and offers his hand to help me up and we limp off, back down Speedway, together.

"This is really what you do for a living?" I can't help it. I'm tired and I can't believe how many dirty places I've rolled in today.

He doesn't really answer me, just shoots me a look and walks ahead a little faster. I guess our moment is over and it's back to him being annoyed I'm even around.

INT. MICHAEL'S OFFICE – A LITTLE LATER

I'm thankfully on the couch now, cup of tea in hand (thank you, Effie), feet safely back in their paper slippers. I have gone quickly through the events of my night, bringing Michael fully up to speed on what I know about Shrek, Ferret, Fatman and the offer for the three-legged cat.

I do, still, leave out the part about my promising to get it or else. I'm just straight up afraid to admit I f'd up to the point it could get us, you know, keeech (think the sound of a knife across your throat).

He listens and nods, and very kindly dabs some disinfectant on a scratch on my forehead, but doesn't say much.

I can never quite tell what he's thinking, which bothers me a little. I'm like totally intuitive when it comes to almost everybody. But when it comes to Michael, I'm just Audrey Hepburn in *Wait Until Dark* (blind).

When I'm through with my recount, there's a moment of uncomfortable silence. I can't stand silence, uncomfortable or not, and feel compelled to lighten the mood:

"Is it me... Or is this a lot harder than our show ever was?"

Michael gives me a half-smile.

"Ha! I *can* still crack you up." I say, pleased with myself.

He dabs again with a bit of force and I wince a little. Now that the adrenaline is ebbing, I can feel how beat up and sore I am all over.

"I need you to sit this out, Kam." He says this very seriously. Very thoughtfully. I actually think he cares.

"But..." I start...

And he stops me with: "I can't do my job if I'm worried about you."

"You were worried about me?"

He tosses the cotton ball into the nearby trash bin and gets up.

"Why didn't you tell me about Alan?"

I'm quite surprised at this turn of questioning.

"How is this important?"

Michael doesn't answer.

"Why would I mention him? You never liked him."

"Not even a little."

"Is that why you quit, when he took over the show?"

"I didn't quit." Michael says with a force that belies some anger running through it.

"What would you call it, then?"

"A lot of things you wouldn't like. Betrayal. Back-stabbing. Walking over a warm body to get to where you want."

I gasp. Those are really things I don't like, especially when it sounds like he thinks I did those things to him.

"Call me crazy, but you sound a little bitter."

"That was my show, Kam. Based on my life. And you stole it. You had me kicked out the door like yesterday's fish wrap, so you could be the star."

I can't believe he would say something like that to me. I am up and off the couch, limping gingerly his way: "I never. I loved us as Polly and Jake."

"Jake and Polly." He says, flatly.

"You walked out on me." I give him a big puppy dog look. I want him to know how hurt I was when he left. He doesn't seem that moved.

"Alan told the network you'd quit if you didn't get the show solo." Michael seems to accusing me of being part of that. But, this is news to me and it takes my breath away.

And then I say out loud something I vowed I would never tell another soul, not even Lumm, because it hurt too much: "Alan told me you hated me because my bad acting brought down the caliber of the show. He said you told the network it was either you or me."

We stare at each other, knowing we both got played, hard.

"Alan." We both say at the same time.

So many years, so many hard feelings and for what, a guy who ended up cheating on me? He's the rat and here, this nice and decent guy, he thinks I'm the rat.

"I didn't betray you, Michael. I'm not a bad person. I wouldn't want my career if it meant I had to walk over you, or anybody."

He looks at me and I know he knows that about me.

"Do I get to hear that? Please. I need to hear it."

"You're not a bad person." He says, as if I have a gun pointed on his dog.

"And you don't hate me…" Oh, maybe that's asking too much, too soon.

"You drive me crazy."

"But, not always in an awful way, right?"

I smile and I think he thinks I look really sweet and cute right now. And darn, the moment is broken by Effie standing in the doorway with an "Ahem…"

"What?"

"There's like one Jocelyn Swanson from Des Moines and she works at a cookie shop in the Moline area. I just got off the phone with her. She's like sixty and sweet and very religious. She's sending us a batch of her special crucifix-shaped cookies. So, definitely not the piece of work who is our client. I also checked David's prison records… No family listed. Our Jocelyn Swanson… doesn't exist."

"Not a big surprise. Good work, Ef. Drive Kam home."

I hold up one finger Effie's way, "Give us a sec."

She nods and futile, but cute, closes Michael's door in an effort to give us privacy. But, with the glass still broken, you know, comical.

"You're going home." He says in an effort to get a sentence out before I start in.

"Okay."

"It can't be that easy." He eyes me, knowing there's more. There is.

"Why were you at the B! interview?"

"I figured, why not?"

"No." I know him better than that. "You always have an angle."

Michael just looks at me, but doesn't reveal anything that I can pick up on. Why is he so hard for me to read?

"I was there…" I am in confession mode now, "because I needed something. Things have been… I don't have much right now. So this case, this working with you, it means something to me. It's real. That's something acting can't give me. I need this, like you don't know."

Michael nods. He can be obtuse, but he's not unkind. "We need to find out more about this Golden Dragon angle. Can you do that?"

I nod, knowing this is a big give for him. I start out and then, I know there's one more thing we need to discuss and it might as well be now.

"One last thing, about the three-legged cat and Fatman… I told Fatman we'd get it for him. I sort of promised."

"I don't see how exactly that's a promise you can keep."

"Yeah, he doesn't really care about that. He just wants it and if we don't get it for him in about forty-five hours, he's probably going to kill us, at least one of us. He kind of threatened both of us. Sorry."

And I brace myself for Michael's anger. He surprises me by remaining calm.

"Well, we'd better get it then." He simply nods and I am so grateful right at this moment to see the softer side of Michael. That went so much better than I expected.

EXT. SHANGRI-LA MOTEL COURT – LATER

The Shangri-La Motel Court is one of those rundown hideaways in Malibu, just off the Pacific Coast Highway, that saw its heyday in the 1950s. It was primarily used by weekenders who wanted to be near the beach. And I suspect, weekdayers, in for some afternoon-delight. I have no idea if that's still the clientele they get here. And I have even less an idea how Jocelyn, whatever her real name is, a girl not from around here, found her way out to a dump like this. I hope at least it's cheap, but in LA, cheap usually comes at a steep price.

As I pull into a space directly in front of Room 21, Jocelyn's room, I am alarmed. The door is open and the place, the entire place, feels weirdly deserted.

I exit my car and approach the room cautiously. I press my body against the wall near to the door and listen. Nothing.

I lean my head around the doorway for a look inside the room. This is always a moment of total fear for me. I know, if somebody is inside, this is the perfect time to either bash my head with something that would hurt, or simply shoot me right between the eyes—which would not hurt that much, but would leave me pretty dead.

A beat. Nothing has come crashing down on me and I'm still alive. I might as well go all in.

INT. JOCELYN'S ROOM – CONTINUOUS

Ransacked. By whom? Looking for what? It's certain Jocelyn doesn't have the cat, or the key to a fortune. If she did, I bet dollars to donuts she'd be long gone, not that worried about her brother, or whatever he is to her.

And looking around, I'm pretty sure, Jocelyn was cleared out of here before the ransack. There is nothing of her few personal items anywhere in the mess. For all I know, she did this herself. But why, what angle is she playing and on whom is she playing it?

I pretty much decide there's nothing here and I'm just wasting my time when I notice on the bed sheet a drop or two of blood. I stand in place and look around and then see on the disgusting shag carpet, a torn, fake nail—the kind I think women call 'fills'. I think they are super-glued on or something. I mean, I really have no idea except I know they are impossible to get off unless you pay for the service, which strikes me as completely stupid since they pay to have them put on.

As I lean down to pick up the nail, I realize the phone receiver is on the ground as well.

It's an old-fashioned corded, push-button phone, circa maybe the 70s. It's got that nice avocado color. Instinctively, I pick the receiver up and place it on the cradle.

I'm startled as the damn thing RINGS the instant it's in place. I watch it RING ONCE, TWICE and then pick it up. "Hello."

There is no answer.

"Is this you, David?" I take a stab in the dark and I must hit some nerve because the voice that comes at me does sound like what I think David might: weasely and frightened.

"Tell him I don't have it! Tell him to leave me alone!"

There's a CLICK and then a DIAL TONE. Okay. Short, sweet and to the point. David is afraid of whom? The guy driving Jocelyn around? The Fatman? Can't be the Mandarin guy. He didn't seem that dangerous. Tell him I don't have it. David must have the three-legged cat or at least, this is what everybody thinks and this is why everybody is after him. This holds the key to the great whatzit. And the great whatzit must be the Golden Dragon, whatever that is.

As I'm piecing this all together, I forget that I'm holding the phone receiver in my hand. I'm about to replace it on the cradle again, when I notice the mouthpiece has not been screwed on cleanly. It's one row of the threading off.

I unscrew the mouthpiece round and yep, there it is, a bug tapped into the line. Sophisticated. New and high tech. Whoever's listening is close by. This kind of transmitter is a short-range doohickey. If they're still listening, they might have a bead on David from this and for sure, if they've been staked out here, they know everything that Jocelyn would have said on the phone.

There are layers to what is going on here and players I don't know yet. I don't like that. Unknowns tend to get you hurt.

As I leave the room, I eyeball the courtyard for cars, or whatever. I see nothing that looks unusual. This does not make me feel better. Actually unnerves me. They're out there, somewhere.

I get back in my car and drive out, one eye in the rearview, in case. And then I am filled with the worry I wish would go away. If they are not here and not on my tail, could they be following Kam?

And I turn the wheel tight, pulling a U on PCH and try to calculate what the fastest route is up to the valley side of Mulholland from here. I think about calling her and realize I never even bothered to ask her for her phone number. I just never thought I would have a reason to call her and I sent Effie home, so, I got nothing to go on, but a memory of a sweet, new-to-look-old, Spanish house that Kam told me she wanted to keep forever.

INT. KAMRYN'S HOUSE – SAME TIME

When Effie dropped me back home, the first thing I did was to take a long, hot, wonderful bath and scrub all the LA street grime from my body. Other than the scratch on my forehead, there is nary of trace on me of the bizarre events that have swept me up in the last 24 hours.

I had to laugh (to myself) when I emerged from my bedroom, showered, shampooed and shiny, that Consuela, who had arrived while I was dressing, simply said "Hola, Missus…" and kept on vacuuming as if this was just a normal day at Casa de Cade. She has no idea about last night and for some reason, I didn't feel like going into it at the moment.

"Hola, Consuela…" I say as I plop on the couch in the great room, happy to be home and out of the storm.

Milo is here working on the computer. When I got home, there was a note from him on my gate, telling me how worried he was about me and asking me to call him as soon as I got home. So I did. I filled him in and then put him to work on the case.

It didn't occur to me then, but now, watching him from behind as he googles this and that, looking for information about the Golden Dragon, I wonder, how did he know where I live? I never told him and the house is listed in a trust, not by my name, and I don't even get mail here (that goes to a P.O. box down in the valley, in Toluca Lake).

I wonder if it's possible, as my biggest fan, he's been following me for a bit. I'm not sure if I find that creepy or cute. He seems harmless enough. His aura is such a lovely shade of blue. I can't, in any way, imagine he's an issue for me.

"Any luck?" I ask, pulling his attention towards me.

"Nothing. I mean, Golden Dragon comes up all over the place, mostly as names of restaurants. But I can't find anything in particular about it and a three-legged cat." He furrows his brow like a man not used to coming up with goose eggs.

"As soon as I get this phone call returned, I'll hop in and help."

He nods and goes back to typing.

I am waiting for Alan's office to call me back. I have called four times this morning. I know, annoying, but as an ex-wife, I feel I can break all sort of codes of decency and get away with it. I am hopping mad about his lies to Michael and me and I want him on the phone to give him a piece of what I'm thinking.

I hate waiting and am not particularly good at sitting blissfully in stillness.

I grab up a tabloid magazine from the stack on my coffee table and breeze absentmindedly through it, skimming the stories about the Kimberlies (a pack of sexy, teen reality stars all named some version of 'Kimberly' and famous for being famous), the hot, new TV season (in a week, most of these shows will fizzle), the movies that bombed last week and what sexy star is turning gay this week (there's always one and usually, after the publicity about it dies down, they switch it back for a second round of the magazine chatter).

The Hollywood of today is such a strange and fake, plastic place. The irony of that reality is, the people in it are, for the most part, quite nice and genuine. Most of us are just kids with big dreams from the small towns smattered across the US, what the coastal elites refer as 'flyover' country. That's a term I don't much like, especially since it's usually used with such an air of mock and disdain. I mean really, don't these people have family who live there? What's with the attitude, I'll never get that.

As for the plastic-life, it's just the shiny veneer that bubble wraps the town. The system gins it all up. And in order to protect yourself, your *real* self, you adopt the plastic personas you think the system wants you to wear and then, you just let the system pretty much do to you whatever it wants (because it's not the real you, it's the plastic you). As long as it helps your career, and pretty much, any notice does, you swim with the sharks.

To win, you have to play the system as hard and as smart as the system thinks it is playing you. As the Abba song goes: It's the name of the game.

We all know it. We all sign up to play it. We all hope

to survive it. Not all of us do, but actually, on balance, I think most of us do just fine. The truth is, it's not as horrible as those living outside the donut hope it is for us.

So reading that magazine took what, fifteen seconds? I pick up my iPhone and hit redial. I don't care that Alan's new assistant is going to tell anybody who will listen I'm some crazy, stalker ex. I need him on the phone.

"Hi, it's Kamryn, again." I say as sweetly as I can be. I mean, I'm not mad at this girl and I don't want to take up an attitude with her. In fact, I'd like to befriend her. Assistants, as friends, are key tools in the Hollywood game and bonus, they often grow up to be bosses. Never diss an assistant—that is just a fool's play.

"No, not Diaz. Do I sound like Cameron Crowe? I mean, you know he's a guy, right? Kamryn Cade. We were married. And make it clear to Alan, I'm not calling about the audition. No, wait… I…"

I'm shocked and look at my phone. The assistant hung up on me. Oh, it's going to be hard to be nice to this one. I sigh.

"She hung up?" Milo has turned and is watching me.

"Either she did or maybe Alan." Pretty sure he's not calling me back.

"Totally unfair of him not to give you a chance in that movie." Milo smiles at me sweetly. I hope some girl likes him. He strikes me as a great catch, or will be when he gets just a little bit older.

"I agree. Hopefully Lumm will have some luck strong-arming him into getting me in the room."

"Does that work?"

"All the time. Just gotta have the right leverage to get the door open." I smile and it's true, leverage is key and right now, I don't have any.

Instead of being mad at Alan, which is just a waste of my good energy, I decide to focus myself on the mystery of the Golden Dragon.

"You haven't found anything?"

"Maybe the thing doesn't really exist."

"You'd think if people are going to get killed over something, it'd be real."

"Not necessarily," Milo points his finger my way, "Remember episode one-dash-nineteen... "

"*The Case of the Monte Cristo Mallard.*"

We say at the same time.

"All those people died and then you found the bird, nothing but plaster and fake glass."

I do remember that episode. I found it sad. "I like the ones with happy endings better." I say, biting my lip, thinking.

I lean over Milo's shoulder, placing my iPhone on the table next to his and scan the Google hits. There is nothing that screams '*Eureka!*' And then, I have an idea.

"Can I get in here?" Meaning, can I take the conn?

Milo gets out of the chair and lets me drive the computer. The first thing I do is change my language and keyboard options to Chinese/Simplified (it's easier than you think). And then I enter the Google search in Chinese characters.

"What are you doing?"

"If the Mysterious Chinese Man is telling the truth,

even a sliver of the truth, and the dragon does belong to him, then the dragon isn't American. Maybe the information about it isn't either."

And with that, I hit enter, and a whole page of Mandarin hits comes back. I click on *Translate* and find we've googled the mother lode of Golden Dragon information.

"Wow." I like that Milo is impressed with my hunting skills.

"Let's see what this says." And I click on the third item down (because the first couple of ones in a Google search return are always sponsored junk).

A picture of a Golden Dragon materializes with a complete PDF backgrounder on the legend of the missing Golden Dragon.

The dragon, in general, in China, is considered a powerful talisman of power, strength and good luck for those who are worthy of it. Emperors, since the first Qin dynasty, adopted the dragon as the emperor's symbol.

There have been many golden dragons over the years, as the yellow and gold dragons were much admired and sought after by the emperors, but there has only been one five-clawed Golden Dragon (five claws, it seems, denotes the dragon to be of emperor quality) to ever have been stolen. This golden dragon was taken from Emperor Gaozu's (of the Han Dynasty) private art collection, and lost to time, but always rumored to have been hidden in private art collections throughout the world. The last rumor had it in Singapore, but that was never verified.

Gaozu's Golden Dragon is the most sought-after Chinese artifact to ever leave the country and considered priceless. Although the PDF does guesstimate an actual worth of about 100 million US dollars.

"One hundred million dollars?" I WHISTLE again. It just seems like the right thing to do when talking big numbers. "Could this dragon be what this is about?"

"It would definitely be worth killing for." Milo says.

The Golden Dragon, I read on, is about one foot long from tail to fire-breathing nostrils and about eight-inches high. As mentioned, it has the five toes on its talons, denoting it emperor-worthy and wings that move and spread out to a wing span of almost fourteen-inches across.

As this dragon was crafted in about 250 BC, moving wings are a miraculous feat of artisanal craftsmanship that had never, to that point, been seen.

This Golden Dragon is actually green, a beautiful shade of deep, dark, jade. It's covered in what appears to be magnificently-detailed, tiny thins of jade dragon scales and it is this bit of artistry that allowed the statue to move fluidly to the delight of the Emperor Gaozu.

The eyes are made of two vivid blood-red rubies which appear to glow in their yellow-back settings. Yellow, because the beast's body is made of 24-carat gold, mined as a gift to the Emperor by his people in the northern province of Inner Mongolia.

"That thing is seriously beautiful." Milo, it seems, might have an eye for art. The Golden Dragon is something to behold.

"The great whatzit."

"One hundred million…"

"Estimated…" I nod my head.

We both WHISTLE. No wonder Fatman would give me a piddly fifty-thousand without blinking a tiny, fat eyelid.

"How does the cat thing fit in here?"

"It holds the key..." I say, thinking it through. "Maybe quite literally."

"Missus..? You have something to tell me?" Consuela enters the room, unmistakably put out, but I'm not sure why.

"Maybe you could give me a hint?"

"You didn't tell me we were having #@!^& company. I didn't make the extra room. I don't have any food in the house. It's all a disaster!"

She throws up her arms and walks out of the great room in a huff. Milo and I exchange a look and then I head for the formal living room at the front of the house.

INT. LIVING ROOM – MOMENT LATER

As I come into the living room I'm quite shocked to see Jocelyn sitting on my couch, all prim and proper, smoothing down her skirt with her ridiculous gloved-hands, suitcase at her feet. She seems to be trying to convince me she's weeping, but I've seen better crying by girls who need glycerin to make it happen.

Why is she such a freak and why can't I put my finger on what's wrong here?

Maybe it's her size, I'm just not used to women who are bigger than say, a size 6 or 8. There just aren't that many of them in the circles I travel in.

Jocelyn looks up at me with her big browns, all moist and needy. That might work on some people, but I'm not on that team and I wonder why she's trying that play on me. I guess maybe sex appeal works for her and she'll use it on anybody. I've seen girls like that from time to time and they surprisingly can go far in this world.

"I didn't know where else to go. Men were at my hotel. They roughed me up." She's acting a scene. I wouldn't hire her. Her performance feels rehearsed. Note to self: Don't do a Jocelyn, shake it up, make it real.

"What would make you think you could stay here with me?"

"I would think, of all people, you would understand how terrifying it is for a woman to have men come to your hotel, push you around. I'm alone in this town. There's nobody to help me."

"What men?" Milo has appeared and enters the room.

"Two thugs, I don't know. Black suits. They didn't give their names."

"We should call the cops." I say, no real intention of doing that, but I want to see her reaction to the idea.

"No... Whatever David's into, now they're after me. Calling the police might make it worse. Is Mr. Barlowe trustworthy?"

This makes me laugh. "More than you are."

"He's the only person who knew where I was staying.

"How did you know where Kam lives?" Milo asks a very good question.

"I called the office. Effie told me."

Man she's smooth, but not that smart. I happened to know that after Effie dropped me, she took the rest of the day off to go visit her grandmother in Pacoima. No chance she went back to the office.

I look Jocelyn up and down, focusing on what she's wearing.

"What are you looking at?"

Good. I'm making her nervous. "I'm not sure, but I think a two-thousand dollar Ann Demeulemeester sweater."

"I don't even know what that means." She doesn't exactly convince me.

I cross to her and pull at the back of her sweater, grabbing at the tag, finding exactly what I expect: an AD brand label.

"Do you just lie about everything?"

"This was a gift. I'm seeing a married man with a lot of money. It doesn't mean I haven't been telling you the truth. I'm in trouble. I just need a place to stay for the night."

"Don't do it, Kam." Milo says, worried.

I eye her suitcase and something in me snaps, or releases or just goes for it. I grab the case off the ground next to her. She makes an attempt to keep me from getting it. I scream at her and act certifiably insane, stunning her and grabbing it away from her with next to no resistance.

Now, I am not a screamer, but I've played some crazy-ass bitch parts in my day and what I admire about these characters—and in order to play them well, you have to find something in them that isn't all bad—their behavior is so outrageous it just freezes people in their tracks, giving the advantage in almost any situation to the crazy mo-fo who's having a freak out. I've never done this in real life before, but I have to say, I'm pleased, it works just as in every scene I've ever played it.

Both Jocelyn and Milo stare at me, mouths open, suddenly a little fearful of me turning on them.

I crack open the suitcase and toss everything she has out on the couch, the table, the floor. So rude of me, I can hardly believe I'm doing it. My mother and every one of my southern ancestors would be appalled. This is clearly a breach of basic, good manners. But part of me wants to make sure she isn't packing a gun or some other thing I might not want staying overnight in my house. She isn't. There's nothing here but her strange assortment of odd tops and old lady skirts and a few, new men's shirts, which I think could probably be for David.

And when I'm done, I realize I'm panting a bit. I catch my breath and nod. "Sure. One night."

Consuela, who is in the doorway of the living room, SIGHS LOUDLY, grabs her purse, mutters in Spanish about going to the grocery store and exits out the front.

I watch her go and I guess a look of worry crosses my face because Milo steps up next to me and very sweetly says: "I'll stay with you."

"No. That's okay, Kid. I got it."

We all turn to see Michael entering from the interior side of the house, meaning he probably came in through the pool's patio entry.

"The pool gate is open. You should lock it."

"The gardeners are coming today."

"Any number of people could be coming today."

I nod. He's right. Suddenly my house has become Grand Central on this case.

Michael looks at Jocelyn in a way that is usually reserved for me, not happy to see you.

He then looks to Milo. "You can go now."

"Oh, okay…I'll just grab my phone."

Milo shuffles out to the great room and half beat later he's heading out the front door.

"Thanks, Milo. I'll let you know if we figure anything out." I say and smile.

"No, you won't." Michael interjects and throws me a look. "We're on a case and he is not a need-to-know part of it. You need to learn some boundaries."

I go quiet, not liking to be sort of put in my place in front of others. I suspect, in the main, Michael is right about that. Milo lets me off the hook.

"It's okay. I'll check in in a couple of days to see if you're ready for those interviews."

"Great." I say as I walk him out. Once the door is closed, Michael hovers over Jocelyn.

"Who rifled your room?"

"I don't know."

"What were they looking for?"

"I don't know."

"What's your real name? And if you say, I don't know, I will slap you."

She leans back and folds her arms. "It's not important. What is, is that I've paid you a lot of money to find David. And it'd be very helpful if you simply did your job instead of harassing your paying client.

"Okay," I say sitting on the arm of the couch. "Now we're getting real."

"David called you," Michael dangles.

"What did he say?"

"He said, tell him I don't have it. Tell him to leave me alone."

Michael says this very slow and measured, watching how each word lands on Jocelyn. I like this delivery, will have to remember to use it in some part someday.

"I have no idea what he means."

Michael stares her down. Obviously doesn't believe her.

From the other room, my phone is RINGING.

"That'd better be Alan…"

I say, running out to get it.

INT. KAM'S HOUSE - CONTINUOUS

As I gallop into the family room, I reach my phone just before I know it's going to head to voice mail. I tap to answer at a distance and breathlessly, and in a way that may be hard to hear me, answer.

I am surprised when a strange male voice flatly states: "We found Swanson. He's at a place called Xanadu Antiques in Burbank."

I just stare at my phone, not quite sure if I should speak or not.

The flat male voice gets worried: "Hello? Milo?"

And then, I look at the phone and realize, it's not

my iPhone. Milo must have taken mine by mistake.

"Jesus Christ. Hang up," says a second voice. And the phone goes dead.

I just stand and stare at the phone unit, trying to figure this out. "Michael… Can you come here a second?"

And a beat later, Michael comes into the room.

"This isn't my phone."

He looks at the phone and couldn't care less.

"It's Milo's. He took mine by mistake."

"So call yours and tell him to come back and exchange them."

"No, you don't understand. I just got a call on it. Well, Milo did and it was some guy who said…" I stop midsentence because Jocelyn has drifted in and is listening to me tell Michael this bit.

"Just give us a sec." I say to Jocelyn and then make an attempt at being somewhat gracious, after all, she is my houseguest, even if I kind of hate her. "Make yourself at home."

I grab Michael by the hand and pull him into my study, closing the door behind us.

He stares at the shrine room, gobsmacked by what's in it—all my Polly and Jake memorabilia.

"This can't be healthy, Kam."

"Not now, Michael. You can mock me later. Swanson's at some antique store in Burbank called Xanadu."

"How do you know?"

"Because whomever called Milo, and thought Milo answered, they told me. They apparently are tailing him, or tracking him or something."

"I knew that thesis sounded fishy. No one in their right mind would do a thesis on Jake and Polly."

"Polly and Jake."

He stares at me, then grabs the phone and pushes at the screen a bunch and makes it all hop around. He gets totally lost in apps and utilities and sighs, beaten by technology.

"What are you trying to do?" I say, taking the phone.

"Call log."

I hit a button and then an app icon. The call log pops up. Each number is simply listed as: *unknown caller*, except one: *Kamryn Cade*.

"I'm the only number he calls that isn't blocked."

"Contacts."

I hit the contact icon and the only contact on the entire phone is: *Kamryn Cade*.

"So either you're his only friend or that's a burner."

"A what?" I don't know the term.

"A burner. A phone used for a scam that you can just throw away after. Whomever he's working with doesn't want to leave a trail."

Jocelyn opens the door. "Something going on?"

"Can you handle her?" He asks me about Jocelyn.

I nod. "No problem." I say, giving her an evil eye.

Jocelyn shoots me back an evil-eyed look of her own. I think it's fair to say, we are not fast friends.

INT. KAMRYN'S KITCHEN – LATER

After Michael leaves, there are a good fifteen or twenty minutes where Jocelyn and I pretty much just exist awkwardly in the same space.

To break the tension, I suggest we go for a swim. It's a beautiful day in the valley, clear, fresh and will possibly get to about 80. Days like this make me love LA and wonder how, when the time comes, will I manage to leave it (I don't really want to raise a family here).

I know people who are not from here think it's all dirty-dinge and concrete, but actually, the greater LA area is filled with foothills, hikes, greenery, wildlife, views to die for from any number of places and is chock-full for hundreds of square miles of the most delightful little neighborhoods. You just gotta turn off any given main street and you'll see, charm all over.

Anyway, Jocelyn reacted poorly to my invitation to swim. I even offered to loan her one of my guest suits. I guess the idea of wearing someone else's suit might have skeezed her out. I only thought I was being polite. I mean, I do happen to know for sure, on account that I did a pretty thorough inventory of her things, that she doesn't have a swim suit in the case she brought.

So while she declined the idea of getting out of those heavy clothes and into the sparkling blue water of my black bottom pool, she did at least take to the idea of getting a little sun. She's out on one of the chaises now, skimming a magazine and looking thoroughly bored.

I'm just happy to have her out of the house for a minute as I've got a bit of detective work to attend to.

I pick up my house phone and dial UCLA's main switchboard number. I googled that number earlier and have just been waiting for a moment when I am alone.

"Hello. Film and TV department, please."

I wait a minute while the operator transfers me.

"Yes, hello... I'm calling to verify a student is enrolled in your department."

I listen as the voice on the other end goes on about privacy and regulations and all the reasons they really can't tell me anything. And then I play my ace card: fame.

"Do you by chance know the show *Polly & Jake PI?*"

The voice on the other end does and then I know I have her.

"This is Kamryn Cade."

I wait as the voice gushes. Letting this moment play. These are feel-good moments and I treasure them.

"Yes. I love *The Case of Minnie the Moocher* too. Wasn't Stephanie Zimbroskie great in that?"

I always make a point to spread the love to our guest cast members as well. We got amazing guest actors. Truly, the success of any show is in the ensemble and that includes those who come and go each week.

I let her ramble a bit more and we dish a little on that awful final season five. I know she's a true fan, because she sounds sad about how the series ended, not with a wrap up story, but by being yanked, midseason, with no real feeling of a finale or, what everybody really wanted, including me, some kind of reunion with Jake.

I look at my watch and feel it's time to move this along. I can tell now, she will eventually do whatever I ask. It's a perk of being known, people will break almost every rule for you. I don't know why this is, but I feel like it's the popular kid in high school syndrome. When people know who you are, when you don't know them, they become weirdly eager to please you. And since it would be rude not to let them, I am always nice about accepting whatever help or freebie they wish to give me. And yes, sometimes like now, I use that to my advantage.

"It's very nice to speak to you as well. Listen, there's a young man who is trying to get an interview with me about the show. I just need to know if he's legit. His name is Milo Farnsworth…"

It doesn't take but a minute and then I have my answer. No Milo Farnsworth in the program. In fact, my new friend at UCLA's Film and TV program checks the entire university's student data base. There is no Milo Farnsworth in any part of the UCLA's student body.

I hang up the phone, bummed. I lean down on the kitchen island, my chin on my folded hand, staring out at the pool. I guess I knew this is how it would go, but I wanted it to be different. I wanted my instinct to be wrong. I truly like Milo.

There is a sound behind me of somebody coming in the kitchen. I start to turn, expecting it to be Consuela returning with groceries and instead of her, it's somebody, I don't know who, because they grab me before I can get any kind of look at them, whip me around, hold me from behind (so they are at least five seven or eight and change because

I'm five-five and at the moment in slippers) and hit me on the head with something that hurts like what I imagine a mace might feel like coming down on your noggin. Just as I go weak in the knees, I remember I forgot to lock the pool gate (dang) and then, everything goes black.

EXT. XANADU ANTIQUES – DAY

I arrived about five minutes ago and parked three blocks over so I could approach without notice and do my usual stand-and-watch before heading in. You'd think I'd be in better shape with all the walking and standing around I do, but the truth is, I realize after two days of chasing people, I need to hit the gym. Maybe give up some of the morning specials, too. But I'm not crazy about giving up things that make the day easier to get through.

So this antique store is on a corner of Victory, the Victory in Burbank that lopes around and leads you into Griffith Park (there's another that runs perpendicular to this one and it's crazy how much confusion there is having two Victory streets in one town.) Behind the store runs a block-long alley. I'm not wild about that. Too many ways for people to come and go.

The store is one of those places that's a mom-and-pop junk yard. They probably spend their weekends trolling local garage sales buying up things people don't want and stuffing their store with those same *people don't want* items and then pricing them double, sometimes triple what they paid for them. Mind you, these are the same items that people don't want and it's the very reason all these antique stores are crammed to the gills like grandpa's creepy attic.

I step off the curb and cross the street to enter.

INT. XANADU ANTIQUES – CONTINUOUS

A string of sleigh bells attached to the swinging, glass entrance door announces my arrival with a gentle Christmasy CHIME. I expect somebody to pop their head out from the back room any minute and am surprised when the door closes and nobody seems to be in the place but me. I stand very still and listen.

All I hear is the HUM of the AC UNIT someplace on the roof and the traffic moving past outside on Victory.

I look around at the old junk and feel like I don't want to touch any of it. There's the usual weird stuff one might think a studio might come looking for just the right creepy movie, complete with a suit of erotic fantasy armor and what I think of as a lobo (the kind of weapon that will give you an instant lobotomy. Sharp and fast swinger). I give that lobo a tug to make sure it's fastened in the prop good and tight and am relieved to feel it's made of a thick plastic. It would hurt if somebody swung it at you, but chances are, you could keep your head. I find that comforting as I turn my back on it and advance toward the back office.

"Hello?" I say warily. "Anybody here?"

"What are you looking for?" a high-pitched voice

calls out. I look around and don't at first see anybody.

"Ah hum. Down here."

I look down and see a man standing in front of me. A very small, old, craggy-looking man.

"Am I invisible?" He asks with a nasty tone.

He sort of is, actually. In the old days, he'd be called a dwarf, but I'm sure if I said that today somebody might sue me for insensitivity.

"What are you looking for? If we don't have it. I can find it. I can find anything."

"David Swanson." I say and then I watch him for a reaction. He doesn't give me any in particular.

"Never heard of him. Should I know him?"

There's a slight NOISE from the back of the room, at the curtain that leads to the back office. Daylight sunbeams through the curtain, catches my eye. I look that way and see David watching me. I push past the dwarf with force...

"Hey!' He yells as he tumbles like a weeble who actually falls down.

INT. XANADU ANTIQUES – BACK ROOM

I come flying into the backroom, flailing the ratty curtain out of my face and find David struggling to get out the back door, but it's locked with some kind of slide chain that he can't undo given his panic. Good, that's what gives me the time to catch him and throttle him.

I grab him, push him against the wall, slug once the gut for good measure. He doesn't fight back, doesn't attempt to defend himself, he just backs away against the door and then he crumbles to the ground, crying like a baby.

"Jeez. Really, David?" I say shaking my head. "You're what all the fuss is about? I gotta tell you, you're sort of a disappointment."

I kick the crybaby to get up (not hard, just to give him the idea to move it along). He thankfully stops the waterworks pretty fast and dries his tears. He's a sensitive looking man, probably enjoyed prison.

"Mr. Barlowe… How did you find me?" He stammers at me.

"Somebody tapped the phone at the Shangri-La. Not gonna be long before there's a party here." I think this is how he's been tracked, but I'm not sure and for that reason, I'm in a bit of a hurry to hustle him out of this location.

"I've got to get out!" He freaks out in a way that I didn't anticipate. Stress, it appears, he doesn't handle well. I decide not to let his crisis go to waste.

"Yeah. But first, you're gonna tell me about some damn, three-legged cat."

"It holds the key to the fortune."

"Yeah, yeah. I got that. Do you have it?"

"It's hidden. I thought I could get away with this. I never will. I need out."

He turns and claws at the door again, helpless. It's pathetic really. All he has to do is relax a second and slide the chain over nice and easy.

"Tell me where it is."

David finally gets the door open, breathes fresh air like a man who's been underwater for five minutes.

He's thinking about running, not that I would let him, but I give him credit for thinking about it.

He turns back to me, "Yeah. You deal with it. The three-legged cat is…"

David reacts to something, stops midsentence to cringe in pain and then slumps over, falling into my arms. And it's then I see an antique, metal-arrow lodged into his back, deep into his key parts.

It's messy, which is never a good sign when something has been rammed into your body.

I look out the back door and can't see anything, but what difference does it make now, as Hillary Clinton might pound on the desk and shrill against the world.

Clearly, the damage here has been sufficient.

David looks up at me, all helpless and dying and whispers something.

"I can't hear you…"

I lean down closer to him and with his last breath I hear him say: "Rosebud…"

David then goes completely limp in my arms and I have to struggle not to drop him.

Behind me there's a noise and I turn, ready for whatever might come my way and all I see is the old, craggy dwarf, terrified of me, or dead David or something.

"Hey. You gotta…" I start, but before I can say : "…help me…," the dwarf has skedaddled.

The last thing I hear is the Christmas CHIME of the front door sleigh bells.

FADE OUT.

END ACT FOUR

ACT FIVE

FADE IN:

INT. KAMRYN'S KITCHEN – LATER

This is the second time today that I have regained consciousness and needed a minute to figure out where I am. Oh, and my head. Let me tell you, this real life PI work, way harder than the TV stuff.

I lay on the kitchen floor for a moment listening to the house. I guess I'm afraid that whoever knocked me out could still be here. I really don't want to be hit on the head again, or worse. I really don't want the worse.

And where is Jocelyn? Has she not noticed I've been laying on the floor out cold? For all I know she was the one who whacked me, except, well, I'm sure it was a man. I can tell by the arms and the force they used to grab me.

I roll up and turn in one motion and am horrified to see my beautiful, classic, white shabby chic slipcover sofa slashed to a thousand pieces like Jack the Ripper just has a joyride through my living room. And I wonder how long it would take a person to do so much damage. I glance at the phone and then check the call log to see when I hung up with UCLA. It was only about fifteen minutes. Wow. These guys work fast.

I look around my house. It's all been slashed and tossed and before I can even muster the strength to go into my study, where I know all of my precious memories have been ripped to shreds, Consuela walks in casually carrying bags of groceries.

She looks around and rolls her eyes. "Don't expect me to clean this up."

"It's not like I threw a kegger..." I say, dragging myself up to full height and steadying my wobbly knees by holding on to the island countertop.

"I don't think this private detective thing is working out for you," she says, looking around the disaster of my house.

"It's a little harder than I thought it would be..." Oy. "Is Jocelyn still here?"

"Nobody here, but you and that man in the pool."

Man in the pool? Consuela leads me through the patio doors and out to...

EXT. KAMRYN'S HOUSE - POOLSIDE

There is a large man floating face down in the pool. A little trail of blood marks a path in the water as he floats gently to the rhythm of the pool sweeper into the good night.

"Oh, Shrek…" I say with genuine sadness. I kneel down on the pool's edge. I'm not sure why, just seems like the right thing to do.

Consuela steps up next to me.

"You know him?"

I nod. "He kidnapped me last night. I actually kind of liked him."

Consuela nods, knows me well enough to not find that odd. "I'm not cleaning that up either." She states flatly.

I look up to see her genuflect and have a moment for the poor guy, then she goes into the house to unload the groceries.

"You want I call the police?"

"Yes, please."

INT. XANADU ANTIQUES– BACK OFFICE

I am doing my best to rifle this office and get out before somebody has the idea to come for me. But since this was the last place David was and there must be some reason he came here, I can't pull myself out of here until I've looked in every possible nook and corner of this crappy place.

I gaze out over the floor and just hope like hell, whatever I'm looking for is in this office.

I hear the SLEIGH BELLS and tuck up against the wall and wait for whomever is coming to come. It only takes a moment and the curtain flutters and… it's Kam.

She looks at the body of David Swanson on the ground and then over to me. "There's a lot of that going around."

She's remarkably cool about a dead body in the place, but I guess, at this point, she's not new to the rodeo anymore.

"How so?" I mumble as I go back to searching.

"Fatman's thug is floating in my pool. Not there getting a tan."

"What happened?"

"Not really sure. I got knocked out. My house ransacked. Jocelyn's gone. I think maybe I screwed up a little."

"Part of the job. Don't sweat it." I'm not interested in making her feel bad. If she knew how many times I've screwed up, she'd run for her life. So instead, I'm all business: "What does rose bud mean to you?"

"Well, usually you need a little more fertilizer to ensure good flower growth."

I shake my head, wrong concept. "It's part of the mystery."

"Everybody knows it's the sled." She says as she begins to look around the office to find some clue.

"Our mystery. It's the last thing David said before he…"

"It's a woman's name."

"Not necessarily."

"No. Necessarily." Kam has picked up a notebook from the office desk and brings it over to me. "She's one of their eBay customers. Look."

So that's how they unload all this junk—eBay. And then I look around the room and see lots of boxes with eBay mailing labels. I find one with Rose Bud's name and address on it.

"Two-twenty-one Baker Street." I read as I rip open the box. All that's in it is a small, white, porcelain figure of a puppy with enormous, over-sized blue eyes, raising one paw. It's unsettlingly creepy, for so many reasons. The things people will buy. I toss it and it breaks. Yeah, I don't feel the slightest bit bad about that.

"That's in Silver Lake. Just off Sunset by the old KCET building."

In our excitement of the eBay puppy find, we didn't listen for the door CHIME, so we missed it (if it chimed at all), and before we knew it, the curtain was fluttering and there was our old friend, Milo.

"Hi guys. What'd you find?" That face is so sweet, for a liar kid.

"What are you doing here?" Kam sounds kind of sad, like this is some boyfriend she's trying to shake.

"I was headed to your house to exchange our cell phones." He holds the one he has up and gives it a friendly shake, he then notices dead David Swanson nearby. "Oh, wow. Holy…"

Milo stares at the dead body a beat, then looks back to Kam. "I took yours by mistake. I saw your car headed down the canyon, so I followed you."

Kam sweetly takes her phone from him, but doesn't hand his back. "I took Consuela's car."

"Oh…"

"Oh is right, kid." I grab him, hard and shove toward the main room. I know just what to do with him. I pick up a roll of packing tape off the desk and shove again.

INT. XANADU ANTIQUES – LATER

After I ran out of packing tape by wrapping an entire roll around Milo, basically bubble-wrapping him to the erotic fantasy suit of armor, I found some twine and did a second round of bondage, just to be sure.

Kam is looking on, feeling conflicted by this, and yet, she's hanging tough as I deal with the kid. We don't want to hurt him, but we don't want him to follow us either. And there's no chance of that by the time I get done tying off the twine.

I signal for Kam that it's time for us to go and she gives the kid one last wave. "Sorry, whoever you are. I really liked you."

The kid nods and mumbles something heartfelt back to Kam. We don't know what, exactly, as the first thing I did was slap some tape over his mouth. But whatever he's saying, you can see in his eyes, he really likes her too.

As we head for the door, it occurs to me that in the hour I've been here not one customer has come in. Gonna be a long time before that kid gets rescued. I got no problem with that.

INT. MICHAEL'S CAR (IN MOTION) – DAY

I let Michael drive us. Not because his car was particularly better-suited for stakeout work than Consuela's (It's not. It's a ten-year-old BMW 5-series, nice, but no real modern bells or whistles. Consuela's is a 2013 Ford Hybrid, fully-loaded, complete with iPod plug-in. It's a sweet ride and a lot of fun to tool around town in), but rather because I know guys. They feel all manly and in control if you let them drive and that's fine by me. This way I can sit and play with the radio, one of my favorite things to do.

As Michael pulls to the curb at Baker Street, about three or four duplexes down from 221, I land on Ambrosia's *That's How Much I Feel*. How lucky am I?

"I don't know how this whole business started… Of ya thinking that I had been untrue…" I smile at Michael as I hit that sweet 70s key. "But if you think that we'd be better parted, it's gonna hurt me, but I'll break away from you-ouououou… Well…" And just as I'm ramping it up, Michael mutes the sound from the steering wheel.

"Are you kidding me? We're on a case here." He sounds disapproving.

"I thought you said we were going to sit for a few minutes and just watch the place. We can't listen to music and watch the place at the same time?"

"Can't you just sit and be quiet?"

"No. Actually. That's really hard for me."

I reach over to turn the radio on at the unit and Michael puts his hand on mine, just for a really nice second and then moves my hand off the radio.

He then checks his watch. I guess he's got some internal sense of how long to watch a place and I gather he thinks we've been in this car long enough to know if anybody is following us or watching the place. He unbuckles his seatbelt, leans across me and opens his glove box, grabbing out a gun and checking to see if it's loaded.

"Just wait here, okay? Let me check it out."

"Yeah, right." I'm half-laughing and then I say, more seriously: "Do you not know me at all by now?"

I unbuckle my seatbelt and get out of the car.

EXT. BAKER STREET – CONTINUOUS

Michael stuffs the gun into the back of his pant waistline and I wonder how come when guys do that, the gun never seems to just fall down their pants. And of course, there's the worry about the damage it might do if it accidentally goes off, which I guess, if I think about it, is why they put it in the back and not the front.

We cross to the west side of the block. This is a sleepy street. Older model cars parked in front of modest duplexes. Tired, unkept palms line the sidewalks and sway gently in the day's easy breeze. A dog rambles carelessly across the street and I watch it, hoping it belongs to some house that is nearby. Somewhere, not far away, somebody is watching *Family Feud* really loud and probably with their front door open.

As we come up near to 221, we get a closer look. It's the top unit of a two-story, old-Spanish duplex, the kind they built throughout LA in the 20s and 30s. It's in really nice shape and I wonder if this neighborhood holds a good turnover price or what it gets for rentals.

It's right on the edge of hipster central, Silver Lake, and probably up and coming. I'm always on the lookout for a good piece of property. That's not always in the A-lister areas. I found a lot of great value in some of the lesser neighborhoods. It's all about what you get in for, what you put in and then, of course, what you can get out. Simple math really.

I look up and down the block and don't notice any for sale signs. I'll have to remember to Zillow this area when I get home later.

Michael puts his arm out and corrals me to a stop and moves me toward the front foliage of the duplex next door. We get a good view straight up the stairs.

"Any chance you'll wait here?" Michael is always trying to get rid of me.

"None."

He nods and leads us up the stairs, stepping very carefully and lightly, hoping not to cause the stair treads to make too much noise before we can get up to the landing and get a peak in through that front window.

It feels sneaky, what we are doing, and I have to admit, my adrenaline is starting to pump. This tip-toeing to the unknown is very exciting stuff.

At the top of the landing, Michael looks in through the window. It overlooks the tiny eating area and right on into the tinier kitchenette. No one is evident.

"Should I knock?" I'm not really sure what the protocol is here.

Michael moves me out of the way, putting himself between me and the door and wraps once, twice, firm and strong.

"Yes?" A little voice comes from the other side of the door.

Michael hesitates, not sure what to say. I am never at a loss what to say (or rarely). I pipe in: "Yes, hello. We're looking for a Ms. Rose Bud. We're from Xanadu Antiques in Burbank."

"Oh…" The door is opened by a small, homely, elderly lady in a housecoat, slippers and shower cap. It's held to just inches open by the slide chain. MS. ROSE BUD puts her face into the breach. Poor thing could really use a serious tweeze session. But I suppose when you get old, those stray hairs, especially the ones in the nose, are just really hard to see.

She looks up at Michael and me. "What can I do for you?"

"David Swanson sent us." Michael says, as he tries to get a look into the unit, putting slight pressure on the door with his hand. The chain keeps the door pretty firmly not open, not inviting.

"Oh, David. Dear boy. I hope he's well."

"Not so much. He's dead." Michael sometimes doesn't have a ton of tact.

"Ahhh…That's terrible." Little Rose seems truly shocked.

"Michael…" I say, chastising him. And then I lean down to Rose's height, which is probably insulting, but you know, it just felt right. "We were wondering if you happen to have a three-legged cat?"

Rose Bud shakes her head emphatically. "No. I don't have any cats in here."

And just at that moment, Michael pushes the front door with a bit of force and the chain snaps and the door swings wide, revealing that the living room has shelves full of those awful puppy figurines with the colored, over-sized eyes, thousands (it seems like) of the little figurines in all sorts of playful poses.

"Lady… You have a serious problem," Michael says surveying the sea of cutesy, white porcelain that fills the room.

Rose Bud puts her hands up to wave at us. "Oh, my figurines. They're not what you want."

"We're going to need to get a look at them."

"I'd rather, no. It's not really a good time for me. I'm just—"

Michael abruptly pushes past the little lady and moves into...

INT. ROSE BUD'S DUPLEX - CONTINUOUS

Rose Bud is now hopping around trying to get in Michael's way to slow his roll.

"I'm going to call the police!" She threatens.

"We just want a look at them." I say sweetly, as if that makes our breaking into this lady's apartment okay. I guess it takes some cojones to do this part of the job well and I haven't grown mine yet. I feel guilty about our duplex invasion.

Michael however, does not share my guilt. He is picking up figurines, and when he's sure they're not a three-legged cat, tossing them onto the ground. Several, so far, have broken.

"Easy, tiger..." I can't believe how brusque he's being and to this sweet, old—

"I'd really like it if you left now," screams Rose Bud in a voice that seems an octave or two lower. I turn to get a look at her.

"GET OUT!" demands a strange, gruff male voice.

Ms. Rose Bud is struggling to get out of that awful house coat and what is under the house coat, a dwarf.

"You..." hisses Michael. "You make an ugly lady."

Not sure why he needs to hurl a nasty at this guy right now... "You know this dwarf?" I'm somewhat shocked.

"Little person." He screams at me.

"I knew you'd be sensitive about being called a dwarf."

"Little person." He screams again and then pulls out a gun and waves it at us recklessly.

"Okay. Okay. Little person!" I say as if this will calm him, but he looks beyond calming at the moment.

The way he is waving that gun is freaking me out. I step back, away and my foot lands on one of those figurines that Michael has been flinging to the floor and I tumble, falling back and hit the end of one of the shelves holding all those creepy puppies.

The shelf, under my weight, see-saws up on the opposite end and the figurines begin to slide, en masse, off the end, like lemmings doing their last run. As they hit the floor, one by one, they crash and break.

"Get away from the puppies, or I'll…"

We never get to hear the 'or I'll' because before the dwarf can finish his threat, GUNSHOTS PING PING into the house, SHATTERING the front window and smashing up figurines on the far side of the room.

Michael and I drop to the floor to find safety from whoever is outside shooting in.

In the chaos, the closet door is somehow jarred and it swings open, revealing the real ROSE BUD, dead, stuffed into the closet. She is a much better looking old lady than the dwarf. Poor thing. Killed, it seems, for her love of eBay puppy porcelain.

"I didn't do that. She was like that when I got here," says the dwa—little person. But honestly, at this point, I kind of don't believe anything he says.

The dwarf stands up and puts his head over the window ledge and fires randomly out and down into the street. I'm sure the neighbors must really appreciate that.

Michael has his gun out and he is peering out the window, but at least he has the good sense to not fire it willy-nilly.

I spot something in the closet, on the top shelf above the hanging coats and jackets and, well, above the very dead Rose Bud, and for obvious reasons, it catches my attention, rivets it actually.

It's a cat, a Chinese lucky cat, the kind you often see near the register of your favorite restaurant or nail salon. This one is white, has wide, friendly, green eyes and bright red highlights in the ears, the collar and on the little cat nails on the feet.

Often these little statuettes have one cat arm that is raised and moves back and forth, as if the cat is waving hello, goodbye. But, on this statue, (which is not small, it's about 8-inches tall and apparently modeled on a Buddha-belly mold), the waving arm has been clearly broken off, leaving behind, a three-legged cat.

I let out an audible gasp, which catches Michael's attention.

I suspect that the dwarf, being so low to the ground, didn't get a good look at the closet shelf. Another injustice to little people. Must suck being so small in a world built for tall people. But I am not going to worry about that today.

Michael looks over as I begin to crawl towards the closet.

He is across the room, miming for me to stay put, take cover, play it safe. I shake my head at him and point and mouth the words: "Cat. Three legs."

Michael follows my finger point to closet, but because of the door's swing, he can't see anything. I point. He shrugs. I point. He shrugs. We're not really getting anywhere this way. So I give up and just start to crawl that way again.

As I am just at the closet's edge, avoiding coming into direct contact with Rose Bud's dead hand, I take a moment to do a small victory wiggle there on the floor and then, in one swift move, I leap up and grab the three-legged, lucky cat in a way I hope the firing dwarf across the room might not notice.

"Hey. What're you doing?" The little guy noticed me after all. So much for that.

Um, not sure what to answer exactly, so I answer nothing at all and just run like hell out the front door...

"Is that a cat?" I hear him yell at no one in particular.

EXT. 221 BAKER STREET – CONTINUOUS

I'm aware as I descend down the stairs that not only are bullets flying my way from the street, but also now one or two from the apartment behind me.

I then hear what must be Michael putting the power punch on the little guy. There's a SCREAM and then a THUD and then a moment later, FOOTSTEPS behind me jamming down the stairs. I know they are Michael's because he's yelling at me...

"Run, Kam, Run."

And I do, for my life…

I'm not really quite sure where to go, so I head for our car, the lucky cat tucked into my two-handed grab that would make any NFL running-back coach proud. Nobody's going to get this from me. Nobody.

"That's my cat!" I hear from behind me and I guess Michael didn't hurt the dwarf enough, because he's up and chasing us.

As I glance back, I'm shocked. He's surprisingly fast and he's gaining on me. He is pulling the trigger on his gun, yelling for me to stop.

Thankfully, all that comes out of that gun is a CLICKING SOUND as the hammer doesn't connect with anything lethal.

Frustrated and pretty darn close to me, the dwarf chucks the gun at my feet. It skitters fast and under my left foot. I actually trip over and darn, flail, as I begin to tumble, the cat goes flying, rotating silently, head over paws…

I look up as the ground hits me, hard, and I roll in a direction opposite of the cat's flight.

When I roll back around, I see the dwarf, arms open, catching the kitty. I'm glad she's safe, but did it have to be him?

The dwarf changes direction abruptly to get away from Michael and is surprised when the Mysterious Chinese Man jumps out of the bushes and trips him.

The dwarf flails and yep, the cat statue goes for

another ride. It's surprisingly buoyant for a hunk of cheap plaster.

The Mysterious Chinese Man whacks the dwarf on the head with his Luger and then turns to follow the three-legged tabby's arc.

He runs into position for an outstretched, one-handed pull down worthy of Calvin Johnson. He takes a moment to secure the prize with a gentle stroke and then he's off and running down the block.

The Fatman appears and stops the Mysterious Chinese Man with just a nudge of his stomach. And the cat is up in the air, in flight again... This time arcing down near Michael.

"Get it!" I yell, as if Michael needs my coaching.

Michael does indeed reel the tabby safely into his arms. He turns to show me he's got the cat and all is well and is surprised to find that I am in a bit of a bind.

Jocelyn is holding me from behind with a gun pointed at my head.

She pulls me forcibly backwards, against my will, so I drag my feet a little bit, making it hard on her.

"I'll take the little pussy cat now." She says in a way that sounds like she thinks she's won this thing. "And I'll thank you for a job well done."

"Do not give it to her," pleads the Mysterious Chinese Man as he moves closer to where Michael is standing.

Michael looks at me, looks around him, aware there is danger on all sides.

The Fatman walk directly towards Michael: "Golden Dragon belongs to me!"

The craggy dwarf stumbles up to the gang, "It's mine."

"Shut up, you miserable losers," hisses Jocelyn.

And I can't help myself, even when somebody is holding a gun to my head. "Wow," I say in my best mocking voice. "You have a real charm, don't you?"

"Don't anger her, Kam." Michael sounds like he might actually care if she were to pull the trigger. That's nice. That thought comforts me a little. Because I am kind of freaking out in the inside, but I will not let Jocelyn see that she's got me scared, in any way.

"Yeah, baby. Be a shame to see your vapid, little, brains blown all over Baker Street."

Vapid? Now that's getting me a little mad. I'm pretty sure Jocelyn is enjoying just the thought of blowing my brains out and I'm not really interested in letting that scene play out. I know I have to do something and do it fast and the only thing I can think to do, is what I've done before, be Polly. She knows how to get out of a jam like this, she's done it every week, on every show we've ever done. My playbook is in the opening credits.

"You don't have the guts. C'mon, Jocelyn, if you have 'em, show 'em. It's put up or shut up time."

And with that, I swing into action, mustering every muscle memory from my years of Pilates and stunt-coaching. I flip Jocelyn over my shoulder with a precise and powerful jerk move that the stunt teams guys drilled into me. She lands on her back, hard, with an uncomfortable thud on the asphalt and it gives me pleasure to see it hurts her.

And just like in the opening credits of my show, her hand actually releases her gun as she absorbs the impact.

I have to kick it though, to get it to skitter away from us, across the pavement. I do a little jump, yell "ha" and go into my martial arts pose, ready to rumble.

Jocelyn turns and stands and does a "ha" of her own, and wouldn't you know it, seems like she knows martial arts as well.

We rumble, matching slice for slice, forearm to forearm, kick to kick, twist and turn to twist and turn.

The guys huddle up into one pack and watch the girl fight, heads nodding, appreciating our skills and our moves.

I'm feeling like I could win this one pretty soon when I get one particularly good kick and twist on the she-goon and knock her to her knees and watch her roll away from me. I only realize, a beat too late, that where she's rolled to is where her gun is. When she's back on her feet, she's got the weapon on me again.

"Uh oh." Is all I can think of to say and I bite my lip, like: Now what?

"Been nice knowing you…"

And I do believe she is just in the process of pulling that trigger when Michael, still holding the cat, flies into the scene, kicking Jocelyn with all his force, in the *whooo-haaa!'*

She folds, turning a shade of pain-filled purple and drops to her knees, dropping the gun as she goes down in a crumpled mess.

Michael picks up the gun. "I just got what David meant when he said, tell *him* to leave me alone."

Then Michael does the most-fantastic-dramatic thing: He gives a hard yank on Jocelyn's hair and pulls off her/his wig.

She is a he, by now you know that. And finally, I get what was with those creepy gloves. Man hands. You can never hide those.

I walk up to Jocelyn and lean over her, looking her straight in the eye. "Don't you know, Polly Parker always gets her man."

And man, does that feel good to say again. Loving that moment... I feel reborn. I taste blood and realize my lip is cut. I wonder too if that pain at my left eye means shiner and I realize, I don't give a damn what I look like. That's how crazy I am right now.

And finally, the sirens come. I turn to see three vehicles screeching toward us, but surprisingly not LAPD units, black sedans. Feds.

And slowly, the neighbors materialize to take a look at what's going on on their street. Several of them recognize me and I can tell, they think this must be a shoot for a movie or a TV show. I can see them looking for the camera, the crew, something that would make this crazy scene make sense to them.

From the back of the last sedan that screeches up to us, comes Milo. He is flashing a federal badge and yelling the funniest thing: "Everybody freeze. FBI! We want that cat."

Milo has a gun drawn and is waving it around at no one in particular. All the other agents have already corralled and cuffed everybody: Jocelyn, the dwarf, the Mysterious

Chinese Man, Fatman and even the tabby.

Oddly, they know enough not to cuff Michael or me.

Milo, still sporting tape and twine, looks around, satisfied this case is under control. He reholsters his weapon.

"You're a Fed?" Michael can't quite wrap his head around it.

"Junior Fed. Still in training." Milo says a little sheepishly.

"I knew it. You're the nineteen on the Glock barrel." I say excitedly.

"Yeah. I'm still having a little trouble with the recoil. I'll get it though." He smiles at me. "I'm sorry I lied to you. They needed someone who knew your show, to get close. I was their guy. This was my first case." He beams.

One of the senior FBI men go by and pat Milo on the shoulder affectionately. "Good job, Milo. This is gonna light up your recommendation."

"I knew you were a good egg. You have the most beautiful blue aura."

"I really do like your show. Sort of the reason I'm in law enforcement."

"Oh brother..." Michael rolls his eyes. "What's the deal with this cat?"

"Well, in theory, it holds the key to a safe deposit box at a bank in Chinatown, where we think the Golden Dragon is being kept."

Milo takes the cat from Michael and shakes it. There is no sound to indicate there's a key inside.

Milo then looks in the hole in the bottom of the cat,

but can't see anything. He sighs, clearly unsure.

I grab the cat from him and say: "Sorry, cat..." and then throw the thing to the ground with all my might, smashing it into a hundred-million specks of white dust. And in the rubble, there is clearly a key embedded in a hunk of remaining plaster.

"Alright, Kam." Milo throws me a smile.
Michael bends down to retrieve the key, brushing plaster pieces from the metal.

"What bank is that key to?" I asked, excitedly. I mean, to think, this is literally the key to a priceless, missing, ancient Chinese artifact that once belonged to an actual Emperor.

"No marks on the key." Michael can't see anything that indicates which bank.

Milo sighs, looks down at the rubble and shakes his head. "Well, I think that information may have been written on the shield the cat was holding. You know..."

I look at the rubble and my heart sinks. "Oh no, what have I done?"

I am on my knees in a flash and am about to start to try and piece the tiny plaster bits into some semblance when I feel Milo's hand on my shoulder.

"Kam. No, wait. I was kidding. It's Cathay Bank... Sorry..." Milo shrugs at me. "I thought that would be a funny joke."

I look up and just start to laugh. Wow, I think. The kid can act. I totally bought it.

"We know it's Cathay, because David told Jocelyn, or whatever her, his, name is... we don't actually know that yet. Well, that's where he stashed it, at a Cathay Branch in Chinatown."

"You sure it's there?" Michael asks, all business.

"We'll know in a little bit." Milo hands the key over to another FBI agent.

"Who gets it now?" Michael asks, getting to the heart of the matter.

"That's not up to me." Milo shrugs.

It's now that I realize my cell phone is RINGING and it takes me a second to dig it out of my pocket.

"It's a Warner Bros. number…" I say breathlessly and then I answer. "Hello? Now? Well, okay. Soon as I can."

I hang up, utterly amazed. "If I can get to Warner Bros. in the next fifteen minutes, I can read for Alan's movie."

"My car has a siren…" Milo offers.

INT. WARNER BROS. - AUDITION ROOM

Fourteen minutes after getting the in for the audition, I am ushered into the room where a bunch of shocked faces are either amazed I made it on time or maybe are reacting to how I look: hair mussed, black eye, bloody, swollen lip and torn clothing.

The town's hottest director, BELLA WHITE is seated next to Alan. She is an awesome woman, very kind and full of encouraging energy. I met her once briefly at an Emmy after-party. Her success in this town is a big surprise to most, in part, because she's a woman. She's also black. News flash, black women don't get handed directing jobs. She's the hottest director in town because she worked her way starting with making lousy B-movies, then pretty good B-movies and then finally, amazing B-movies that made money, lots and lots of money.

She's a hoot to talk to. She speaks often of liberation politics and peppers her conversations with a lot of 'yeahs', 'I dig its', 'I feel ya's', and my favorite, 'true that's'. She is, in my opinion, truly groovy. I suspect it's, in part, because she gives off the impression she's constantly high. I don't know if she is, or if it's just an act. It doesn't matter, it works for her. And to be in one of her movies is a big break for any actor, especially one like me, who's career is deader than dead. Getting this part, no matter that it's just a small part, would put me back in the game.

I am handed pages, expected to just literally read for the part since I didn't have any real advance notice.

I'm jumpy and still full of adrenaline from Baker Street and the Wild Mr. Toad's ride over here in the siren-blaring Fed car (that was pretty darn awesome). So much is happening really fast to me and I love it, thrive in the chaos of it.

As I'm scanning the pages, I can hear Alan doing a crummy, half-hearted introduction of me to all the players at the producer's table and telling them I'll be reading for the part of Vivienne.

He's pouting and I know him well enough to know that his baby pout means he's having to do something he really doesn't want to. I smile and look up, pretending to be listening, but really I'm wondering, if he sounds so miserable to have me here, why did he make this happen.

When Alan is done, I'm surprised to hear Bella's easy drawl. "I'm sorry to interrupt your process, Kam-baby, but I have to ask you a question…"

I look at Bella. "Sure. No worries."

"Are you bleeding?" She indicates around my mouth.

I touch my lip. "Maybe just a little." And then I lick the blood away and go back to quickly scanning the pages.

I can sense my energy is way, like drug-ho high. I can barely keep still, am not actually sure I'm not fidgeting in place as I quickly learn my lines.

I know Bella is watching me and I guess she's not totally against me because I hear her say to Alan. "I like her energy, man. I dig her."

I flick a look at Alan and he's totally wondering where is the old Kam and who is this standing in this room.

"Are you okay?" He asks, genuinely wondering the state of me.

I fold the pages in my hand. "I'm good. I'm ready. Let's do this. Bring it."

I'm ready as I'll ever be here.

Alan, it turns out, has been elected to read with me. Bad choice. Writers are horrible to read their own work with. But today, I'm not going to let anything get in the way of my read, not even Alan's dreadful, mumbling incompetence in reading his own script.

"Okay. Hey, Vivienne. What are you doing there?" Alan reads like a fourth-grader.

"Nothing, Steve. A little barn cleaning. Winter's coming. Always so much to do down on the farm."

I stop and look down. There's more to this speech and the writer's note is I'm supposed to read it quietly, like I'm distracted, my mind far away from this moment, this place. This is just awful stage direction. Usually I try to do what they ask, but today, I'm just not in the mood to do another awful audition.

"I'm sorry..." I hesitate and consider going right back to the scene, just to play along and not rock the boat.

Hollywood hates boat rockers. But something in me rises up and, here goes: "Come on, Alan. She's just killed her neighbor, ground him into little bits and is trying to hide the evidence. You write her all calm and molly-sweet! That's crap."

"Well, I…" Alan stammers and is interrupted by Bella.

"True that. I have bumped on that myself."

"Bella-baby, if I may…"

"Right on…" I get for encouragement.

"She'd be wired. Just twenty minutes ago I was having a knock-down, drag-out fight with a he-she and nearly got my head blown off and right now, I am so totally amped. I have so much adrenaline going through me. I can honestly say, I know what it feels like to kill somebody. And this… (I hold back a mean word here), ain't it!" I say tossing Alan's pages to the floor.

"I like your energy, Kam. Raw. I feel ya." Bella is nodding her head. I'm glad she doesn't seem offended.

"Alan, sorry, this is, it's hack stuff. And you know what, I don't need another bad part. I've had enough bad parts to last a lifetime. When you write something good, no, *great*, call me."

For once, I don't bother with the crap part. I just turn and exit and feel what I haven't felt in years after leaving an audition: Great.

EXT. WARNER BROS. LOT

I emerge from the executive offices to find Milo and Michael milling around the parking lot at the end of Warner Way. Milo spots me coming towards them first, is alarmed, probably by the fact that I've only been in there about five minutes.

"What happened?"

I pause a moment, trying to think how I might frame what just went down and then, well, it hits me what just happened: "I got my confidence back."

That's what I'm feeling, like, not a loser. This is an awesome feeling, very empowering. I've missed it.

"Yeah. And it allowed me to see that part was a piece of yuck."

"Good for you." Michael says, somewhat misunderstanding the moment.

I suspect he thinks I've suddenly come to realize acting is for losers. I haven't, just that taking loser parts is for losers. But there's time to explain that later. For now, I'm just interested in getting out of there.

"C'mon boys, let's hit the bricks and get something to eat. I'm starving."

We three turn to move to Milo's car when from behind, I hear:

"Kam, Kammie, baby..." Alan moves fast in his writer/producer uniform-approved shoes (which I have never liked), his slip-on, sockless loafers, to catch me.

I barely turn and what little of me does, telegraphs

total disdain. "I don't want to hear it."

Panting, Alan stops near me. "She loved you."

Okay, I'm weak, I turn to him completely. "Well, I could hear a little more of that."

Michael and Alan exchange wary looks, but no niceties. In fact, Alan looks a little afraid of Michael, shies away from him and pulls me a step towards him by my elbow.

"You were... great. What's gotten into you?"

"Me. I think." And then... "You bastard. How could you tell Michael I wanted him off the show? Or me, that he quit? What the hell were you thinking?"

Alan looks at us both. The secret's out, no need to shade it anymore. "I was thinking I didn't much like the chemistry you two had, so I took care of it."

Now, it's Michael and I who exchange a look.

Milo doesn't help the moment with: "It was great chemistry. Best part of the show."

"Can it, kid." Michael warns him.

"Right." Milo nods.

"I'd say I'm sorry, but I'm not." Alan, at least, is man enough to be honest with us—now. He's not a total weasel. I take some comfort in that.

"Well, don't bother. It wouldn't be good enough. But... getting me in that room, that's a step toward redemption. Thank you. I could tell, you didn't want to do it."

"Yeah, well, I don't appreciate being blackmailed for it."

"That sounds a little dramatic. Lumm's not exactly a Soprano."

"Alicia? I don't know why you're mentioning her. It wasn't her."

"No. It had to be her. She was trying to get me in…"

"All I know is, I got a call from the FBI. Threatening me with a Homeland Terror Audit, whatever the hell that is. Since when do you or Lumm have friends at the FBI?"

Michael and I swivel little looks at Milo, who's looking away, trying to be a little invisible here, pretending to be examining the large mural of the WB cartoon characters that covers the front of Stage 2's north end, prominent at the Barham/W. Olive turn.

"I have friends in many places, Alan. You should remember that."

"I know. Everybody loves Kamryn Cade. Including Bella. She wants you for the movie."

"Really?"

"I'm standing out here begging you, aren't I?"

"That much?"

"Don't make me grovel."

"I won't. But here's the deal. I'm going to need script approval."

"Oh, Kam…"

"And, I'd really like an Arri lighting package, with egg crate and double wide scrims. Panavision long lenses whenever possible."

"This is Bella White. You can't tell her what lenses to use."

"Does she want me or not?"

"You're killing me."

I smile. Loving that for one tiny moment in my career, I have a wee bit of power. I like it so much I'm thinking as soon as I can, I should move into the producer ranks.

"And…"

"No more 'ands'."

"We'll have to work my shooting schedule around my cases."

"What?"

Both Michael and Alan stammer that out at the same moment.

"Okay. Our cases." I smile to Michael then tap Alan on the forearm. "My people will call your people. I know this deal will make. Ciao, baby."

I grab Michael by the arm and then pull Milo along as well, leaving Alan standing in our dust, dumbfounded as we literally walk off into the sunset. Literally, because there is drive-in size screen backdrop right here of the most beautiful Hawaiian-style sunset that we are passing by on the way to Milo's car.

"That was a joke, right?" hopes Michael.

"We had a deal." I am firm about this. "We solved the case together. We partner."

"You're supposed to go away forever."

"That was if you solved it without me. Do you think he solved it without me?" I turn to Milo for support on this point.

"No. Totally a team thing."

"Shut up, kid."

"I'm just saying it like it is." Milo shrugs.

"So," I go on. "I'm keeping my car. You can keep your office. And I'll order new stationary on Monday."

Michael is about to say something, something I know I won't like. I can see it cross his face before it comes out of his mouth.

"I reject your negativity… partner."

I then turn to Milo. "What do you think of Cade & Barlowe Investigations?"

"Love it." He beams.

"Barlowe and Cade," grunts out Michael.

"That's good too. Either way. I just love that you two will be working together again."

"Me too." I say, with a wink towards Michael.

And as we walk off past the sunset, I lean my head back and laugh. "I believe this is the beginning of a beautiful friendship…"

And with this, we FREEZE FRAME on the happy trio, well Kam and Milo are smiling and Michael looks like he could cry.

FADE OUT.

END ACT FIVE

TAG

FADE IN:

EXT. MICHAEL'S OFFICE - MORNING

Monday morning. I'm not too early, because I'm not really a morning guy. I pull into my one, dedicated spot off Speedway, into my building's overhang parking and turn my car off. I sit for a beat and realize how surprised I am that I haven't heard from Kam since Friday.

I get out of the car and walk around the building to enter through the front door. I stop for a minute, like I do every day and just glance at the beach and breathe in the fresh, sea air. I love this place, everything about it. I love the constancy that it's been this way since my grandfather's day. The world can change, grow coarser, little liars getting ahead while the good guy falls behind, but here in Venice, at this beach, at Barlowe Investigations, we hold the line.

INT. MICHAEL'S OFFICE – STAIRWAY

My office is on the second floor. There is an elevator and for years I have just mindlessly taken it each morning.

I have decided, now, going forward, after all that chasing last week, I had better get used to taking the stairs. So I'm walking it.

After we left Warner Bros., after that thing with Alan, we headed over to this little breakfast place in the Von's strip mall on Pass Avenue, BeaBea's, which is hands down the best breakfast joint in Burbank.

Hanging out with Kam and the kid was weird. They are fast friends already and I felt a little like a third-wheel. I didn't care. I don't really want to be in their little world.

You should have heard Kam go on about all her plans for the agency. That girl thinks on speed. I've always found it hard to keep up. And I've found there's really no need. She moves from point to point so fast, even she forgets half the things she blathers out.

Actresses. Such a strange tribe. I will say this, they are, as a type, exceptionally bright and full of tremendous creative energy. It's really quite impressive, as long as that energy is not aimed at you. When that happens, get out of the way, the tornado could be coming.

Or not. Because another attribute of the actress tribe is, they often flake. They talk a good game, make grand plans and then, well, something else comes up and they totally forget they intended to change the world. Pedicures, facials, massages and auditions can easily distract them. Throw in a sale at some place on Robertson and you can pretty much dodge the actresses' good intentions.

Knowing this, I let Kam talk it all out, hoping that by talking about it, she'd burn out all her actual energy to do anything specific.

Let's be honest, what I do, it's not that glamorous. Decidedly unglamorous and I like it that way. I don't really see the pull for her.

So the rest of that breakfast wasn't all misery for me. There was a lot of laughter and Milo gushing over his love for Kam and our show. And it was sort of amazing what he knew about each episode.

He and Kam spent the hour discussing plot by plot points. I don't remember any of that stuff and listening to it all over again, I felt like I was hearing about somebody else's life, not my own.

It's amazing how Kam lives for the sort of recognition that Milo brought to the table. She lights up for it. It's not a bad look on her, that kind of happiness.

INT. MICHAEL'S OFFICE HALLWAY

As I come out of the stairwell, I pass a glass man who tips his hat to me as he gets on the elevator. I look down the hall and think, Effie got the glass on the doors replaced. Good start to a Monday.

There's a worker standing in front of my door and

as I draw close, I can see he's penciling on the glass.

"What are you going to write there?" I say, drawing up to the door.

"Cade & Barlowe Investigations."

A beat. "Barlowe & Cade," I stammer back.

"Yeah, she said you'd say that. I was just kidding you. Barlowe & Cade, sure."

"How about just Barlowe Investigations?"

"That doesn't seem quite fair to Ms. Cade."

"What's that to you?"

"Well, she is the one who's paying me double my rate to do this today."

"I'll double her double if you do it my way." I say, wondering how much his rate is and knowing, no matter what, I couldn't pay the tab.

He sighs. Not sure what to do. "Why don't you and she talk this out. I can wait. I don't mind. I'm working by the hour and since I'm a studio guy, I'm bagging union rates. So go ahead, take your time." He indicates with a wave of his hand I should go inside.

"She's here?"

He nods and steps out of the way so that I can open the door. So much for hoping she would just go away. What's that saying? If it weren't for bad luck, I wouldn't have any luck at all...

INT. MICHAEL'S OFFICE – FRONT AREA

As I open the door, I'm hit by the smell of fresh paint and then smashed in the face by brightness. I am instantly disoriented. My office is a lot of things, but fresh and bright are not usually those things. Effie comes over to me, giddy. I have never seen her giddy.

"Isn't this great?" She means the new shade of what, to my horror, might be adequately described as vomitous butter cream.

I can also see that all the old packing boxes which I had carefully lined up on the far wall of the outer office, the ones that contain years of my files, are gone and in their place, rows of very expensive-looking file cabinets, not IKEA quality, but a whole wall of real, solid, cherry wood cabinets. Classy looking. That must've cost a freaking fortune.

"Where is she?"

"In her office." Effie says point to the door just adjacent to mine.

"The storage room?"

"Not anymore. Wait until you see it."

I put my things down and head that way, but before I can get there, she comes out.

She is dressed in something that I think reminds me of Patty Duke back when she was on that identical twin show. Her hair pulled back by some kind of simple band. Her shirt and pants, slimming and retro. This must be her 'Barbie-working-Kam' look.

"Michael! It's about time. I've been here since eight. Do you always come in this late?"

"We need to talk. What are you doing here?" I scan the place, my anger growing, calculating how long it will take me to get it back to the way it was.

"Remodeling. The place was kind of drab. Really

needed a little up-do."

"I like drab."

"Yes, but now you have two women here and we don't. And, clients don't like drab. Clients want bright and pretty and new materials like tile, stone and glass. I have my designer working up some drawings for a pony wall entry with a whole new..."

"No."

"Just let me—"

"No. And I don't care what clients want. I barely have any."

"That's going to change. I had my publicist run a little item about us and the Golden Dragon mystery... Effie, what's the distro list on that article?"

Effie grabs a sheet off her desk. "*The Tolucan Times, Santa Monica Observer, Canyon Crier, Beverly Hills Gazette, Silver Lake Today, the LA Times, US Magazine* and maybe *Star*, we're still waiting for a confirm on that."

"Wow." And I'm pretty floored. That's an impressive list.

"Polly and Jake together again. Trust me. Clients will come."

"Are you really doing this?"

"I am. You'll see. It won't be so awful. You might even grow to like me, a little bit." She smiles sweetly. I find her maddening.

I pull Kam to the side, away from Effie. I just want to say something in private. I just have to get to the point of what's really bugging me.

"Kam, look, I appreciate what you are trying to do

here, but, I really can't afford all this."

"Yes, you can."

"I really can't." It pains me to have to insist on this.

"Look, I know things have been tough for you. Effie showed me your books. They're in shambles. Have you no idea how to run a business?"

"Money's not my thing."

"Apparently. But you're in luck. It's mine. I'm great with money. I've doubled everything I made on the show and more."

"Really? How is that possible? I don't have any of it left."

"I guessed as much. Real estate mostly. And I pulled out of the market before the crash. Was all cash until I found a little internet start up to angel invest in."

"I can't take your money." I say warily.

"Wouldn't expect you would. And you don't have to. You have a good bit of your own."

"You find something hidden in the walls?"

"In my office, actually."

"The storage room?"

"Wait till you see it."

Kam opens the door and we enter into:

INT. KAM'S OFFICE - CONTINUOUS

What for forty years had been a small, dark, dingy storage room of about six by eight was now a large, bright, spacious office about eight by fifty, with wrap-around windows that overlook the beach and the street side of the building.

There are workers here, painting, putting up shelves, building partition walls and framing a new doorway that leads into my office.

"I blew out the wall and took over the office next door. And who knew, there were boarded up windows in this space? And here, I'm adding a doorway so you and I can confer without having to leave our desks. Isn't that great?"

"You can't just blow out a wall and take over that space?" I stammer, utterly thrown.

"Sure I can. I had breakfast with the building landlord yesterday, showed him a little sketch I proposed and signed a lease for the additional space."

I am stunned. "A lease? That sounds well, sort of permanent." I just look around at the commotion, beaten by her sunniness. I am only shaken out of this stupor by a lucky cat statue sitting on her desk.

"Was is that…?"

"Our own Maneki-neko. You know, Lucky cat. Turns out, this is actually a Japanese symbol of good luck. It's often called the 'beckoning cat' on account of this one paw waving back and forth.

Kam pushes on the paw which must be spring-loaded as it begins to move back and forth as if the stupid cat is throwing an imaginary baseball.

"I hate cats…" Is all that comes to mind.

"Well, not this one. This is also known as the money cat, the happy cat and the good fortune cat. These are great things for our office. And besides, it was a gift from Milo."

"He's been here?"

"He's here now. On the balcony."

"This building doesn't have balconies…"

"Well…" Is all Kam kind of stammers at me and then she smiles and we both turn as Milo enters the room, I guess from the balcony.

"That is one awesome view." Milo exclaims, as he comes in from the far end of the new space. "Michael, my man. How's it hanging?"

He tries to high-five me and I just stand there and stare at him.

"What are you doing here?"

"He's the good news." Kam says.

"I could use some." I say dryly. This morning isn't making me feel all that good.

"Tell him." She nudges Milo.

"So that key opened a box which did indeed contain the Golden Dragon."

"We're thrilled. Yippee." I say with my usual whimsy.

"Michael… Don't be a sourpuss. In a minute you will regret it."

Kam gives me a look and I swivel a look over to Milo.

"Why? What's going to make me regret it?"

"This might…" Milo turns to the balcony. "Mr. Wei?"

The Mysterioua Chinese Man who is, apparently, MR. WEI, sticks his head in from the balcony doorway and smiles.

"Ah, Mr. Barlowe. How nice to see you again." He comes my way. He looks happy and not at all mysterious anymore. He just kind of looks like somebody's Chinese dad.

"We have been waiting for your arrival." He says as he places a large, old, ornate box on Kam's desk. I know enough to guess what's inside.

"Is that it?" I say, pointing at the box. "It's not as big as I thought it might be."

"Don't mind him, Chaoxiang, he's slow to embrace what is truly great." I hate that Kam is always making up excuses for me. I wish she'd keep her trap shut, at least where it comes to describing things about me.

"Smart men observe first, and talk little. I sense Mr. Barlowe is in that category."

He smiles my way and bows slightly. This guy, I decide, is okay.

Mr. Wei begins to push what appear to be secret, hidden and extremely-intricate, lock mechanisms (like the kind that might cut your fingers off if you got this sequence wrong) in order to release the box's ancient security measures. Not sure how he knows how to do this, what to push, you know, 'cause it seems complicated.

"Chaoxiang…" Milo explains to me, "Works for Minzu University in China. He chairs the Department of Anthropology."

"Fantastic." I say, not meaning it.

"Yes, but right now, I am on assignment for the government." He says as he concentrates on the exact nature of the lockset he is manipulating.

"He's kind of like their version of Indiana Jones." Kam enthuses, always happy to put some Hollywood spin on everything "He specializes in retrieval of historic artifacts. He travels the world, tracking them down. Doesn't that sound amazing?"

Kam throws a smile at Chaoxiang and he throws a smile right back at her. I wonder, when did they have the time to become such buddy buddies? Don't forget, just a few days ago, this guy said, if he'd had to, he'd kill us.

"Ah, here we go…" And as he finishes this sentence, he pushes in the last secret mechanism and the top of the box magically opens on its own, a platform within, automatically rising, revealing what appears to be a sleeping, golden dragon (which is actually jade green), nestled into a bed of comfy deep, crimson velvet.

"Wow." Kam is all wide-eyed and excited like a little girl at Christmas. And while usually I like to mock her for her over-dramatic excitement at the stupidest, mundane things, I gotta admit, there is something about that dragon that catches your breath.

Mr. Wei dons white gloves and then, very respectfully, picks up the dragon. As he lifts the thing off its sleeping bed of velvet, the most cool thing I have seen in a long time happens: The eyes open, revealing those vivid, blood-red rubies Kam told me about. It's startling and Kam actually 'ahs' and backs a step up as Mr. Wei brings the dragon around to show us more closely.

"Wow." Milo exclaims. "How does that work?"

"The eyelids are crafted from curved jade and retract when weight is taken off the dorsal portion of the statue."

He angles the dragon and points to a very small pressure point on the stomach. I guess this is what triggers the eyelid movement. Man, that's scary-effective and to think that some guy living in a Chinese mud-hut hundreds of years ago figured that out. Pretty impressive.

Mr. Wei then articulates just one wing outward and the other follows in the same fashion. As the wings widen, the back feet move forward, revealing the five-claws on each foot. The dragon now appears to be in flight.

"What a beautiful bird." Kam reaches for it with... "Can I hold it?"

Mr. Wei pulls it back from her. "No. I'm sorry. I can't take that chance. She is my responsibility now. I must take care that she gets home quite safe."

Kam, who is never told 'no' about anything (except maybe she gets a lot of 'no's' about jobs), doesn't try to sweet talk him, or smile him to death. She just nods her head, retracts her hands. "Of course. I understand."

Mr. Wei begins to gently and carefully return the dragon to its sleeping travel position. "My country is ever so grateful for your help in the finding and returning of Emperor Gaozu's missing dragon." He turns and smiles at me and does a little head bow my way as he tucks the dragon into the velvet. I'm not really sure what to do, so I kind of give a little head bow back his way.

I hate that out of the corner of my eye, I see Kam smile at my motion.

"I'm just glad it didn't get me killed." I give a shrug.

"I would not have really killed you for it. Mr. Lin perhaps might have."

"That's Fatman's name." Kam interjects.

I just nod her way.

"I was quite certain I could get it without going to that extreme. And since I am on a diplomatic mission, I didn't not wish to cause harm to our countries' current great and wonderful friendship."

"This how the FBI got into this?" I ask Milo.

"Yeah. We were alerted to give Mr. Wei whatever back up he needed. We've been on this for a couple months now as he trailed the shipment and tracked it through Peter Lorring to David Swanson and its arrival here in Los Angeles. We just didn't know where it went once it got here."

"How did it end up with Rose Bud?" Kam has to have every, little detail buttoned up. Once a case is solved, I don't really care for the nitty-gritty. But I suppose it's a good thing to note, for the file.

"Turns out, Mrs. Bud was Lorring's aunt. He sent her the lucky cat for safe-keeping." Milo tells us.

"Well, we no longer care how our dragon got here or what adventures it had in Los Angeles." Chaoxiang says with a smile. "We now only care that it is leaving today, with me, and will be home in China in less than a day's time." Mr. Wei closes the box back up, nice and tight. "Ah, but one last thing, for you, Mr. Barlowe."

Mr. Wei pulls out a large, ornate paper check from his breast pocket. It's very colorful, decorated in what appears to be pictures of ancient Chinese warriors. He hands it to me.

I look it over carefully. I'm pretty shocked that it

reads a six-figure sum: $100,000.00. I gulp. "What's this?"

Kam smiles at me. "That's what happens when you put a lucky cat in your office."

"You were the one who was last holding the three-legged cat. You were the one who handed the key to the FBI. It has been determined by council, therefore, that you are the finder of the missing item. My country is in your debt for your assistance in the return of our most precious artifact."

I simply nod. Pretty stunned. This is one hell of a sweet finder's fee. "Thank you."

"No, Mr. Barlowe. I thank you. China thanks you." He steps forward, removes his glove and offers his hand to shake. I take his hand and we give each other a nod as we shake on it.

Mr. Wei turns to Milo. "I must be on my way to the airport."

"Yeah." Is all Milo says and he nods. "Okay. Well, I guess my work here is done. If you guys need anything, I'm at the Federal Building now. Don't hesitate to call. Really. If you have a case and I can help…"

"I will definitely call you." Kam puts her arm around him and begins to walk them out.

As Milo is about to head out, I extend my hand. "Thanks, Milo. You've been okay."

It's nice the way the kid seems shy about shaking my hand. And then he, Kam and Mr. Wei exit, Kam playing the host and walking the guests out to the front door.

I remain standing in the damn biggest and brightest storage room I've ever seen (I'm not going to call it her office) and I'm holding the damn, biggest, single check I've ever seen. I WHISTLE low. This is what I used to call show money. Big checks. I haven't seen this kind of money ever one check with my name on it, not even during the heyday of *Polly & Jake* money.

I hear the front door open and close and in a beat, Kam is striding right back into the room.

"Wow. How amazing has this Monday been?" She says as she snatches the check from my hand. "You will not be playing poker with this. And, in case it comes up, Simon and Benny have been paid, in full, including a make-good on that rubber check Jocelyn bounced on you. I will deduct that from your half of the fifty-gees."

"Half?" Oh no…

"I am your partner…" She gives me an eye-roll look. "And gosh, Michael, don't you know to never go all in with queens? There's a reason they're called the crying ladies."

"What do you know about poker?"

"Play me sometime and I'll show you."

The way she smiles at me, I'm sure she's good, would take me to the cleaners. Then again, that's not really that hard.

Kam spies the (new) clock on the wall. "I've got to go. My call is at noon. I'm starting Alan's movie today. But don't worry, I'm only booked for seven days. This shouldn't interfere with our cases at all."

She begins to gather up her things, her purse (which is huge and I wonder what she is carrying in it) and a side bag full of heavy magazines.

Of course, I stand there and I say nothing. Because

I have no idea what to say that might actually get through to her.

"Hold the fort." And she heads out.

"Kam…"

She turns back and we have a moment, a look. And because I can't think of just what exactly to say, I just give her a nod.

She nods back.

"We'll see how it goes." I mutter at her.

"Yes we will…partner." She gives me a genuine smile and I have to say, I've always liked her smile. A lot. She's a girl who radiates warmth.

She played it cool as she left, but I know, when she got to the elevator, she did a little victory dance.

FADE OUT.

THE END

NEXT ON:

The Kamryn Cade Mysteries Series

Kam gets a **Dose of Reality** when Michael, in an effort to get her to fail and quit, lets her handle a case on her own.

Kam is hired by a producer friend to hang with his red-hot reality stars, the Kimberlies (five twenty-something girls who are all named 'Kimberly', who are famous for being famous) during the shooting of their TV show: *Keeping Up With the Kimberlies.*

Someone, it turns out, is trying to kill a Kimberly—It's just not clear which one, or why and when Kam becomes part of the posse, she becomes a target as well.

And of course, hanging with the Kimberlies makes Kam red-hot in the media too. Suddenly, Kam is in the middle of everything, including murder. It's a race against time to figure out all the girls' secrets and why one of them is worth a killing for.

You can email Kam at:
KamrynCade@gmail.com

ABOUT THE AUTHOR:

Nan Hagan is a TV writer/producer who has written for such shows as *Sliders, JAG, Dawson's Creek,* and *Diagnosis Murder.* She first wrote *The New Adventures of Sam Spade* (renamed along the years as *Play it Again, Kam*) in the late nineties and took it around town every few years, pitching it as a one-hour series.

After all these years, pitches, meetings, notes, a producer attachment and two-actress attachments to the material, Nan finally decided to take the advice Kam's friend gives in the book: "...*just do it, don't let anything or anybody stop you.*"

So, here is her debut novel, *Play It Again, Kam,* (Book 1 in The Kamryn Cade Mystery Series) which Nan always knew in her heart would make a great series, TV or otherwise.

Ms. Hagan lives in the greater Los Angeles area (valley-side) and when not writing her mystery novels, runs an editorial agency that specializes in coaching writers on the art and development of scripts and novels.

You can email Nan at:
nan.hagan@hollywoodwaymysteries.com

<u>PLAY IT AGAIN, KAM</u>
designed using Adobe InDesign
cover and interior design by:
THE EDIT AGENCY, Burbank, CA
www.theeditagency.com
front matter & interior text: **Adobe Caslon Pro**
front matter titles,
interior act headings, fades & scene headings:
American Typewriter
page numbers: **Apple Chancery**